# GAUDENZIA, PRIDE OF THE PALIO

## OTHER BOOKS BY MARGUERITE HENRY

*Album of Horses*
*Benjamin West and His Cat Grimalkin*
*Black Gold*
*Born to Trot*
*Brighty of the Grand Canyon*
*Brown Sunshine of Sawdust Valley*
*Cinnabar, the One O'Clock Fox*
*Justin Morgan Had a Horse*
*King of the Wind*
*Misty of Chincoteague*
*Misty's Twilight*
*Mustang, Wild Spirit of the West*
*San Domingo, the Medicine Hat Stallion*
*Sea Star*
*Stormy, Misty's Foal*
*White Stallion of Lipizza*

# GAUDENZIA, PRIDE OF THE PALIO

## MARGUERITE HENRY
### Illustrated by LYND WARD

ALADDIN

NEW YORK  LONDON  TORONTO  SYDNEY  NEW DELHI

This book is a work of fiction. Any references to historical events, real people, or real places are used fictitiously. Other names, characters, places, and events are products of the author's imagination, and any resemblance to actual events or places or persons, living or dead, is entirely coincidental.

ALADDIN

An imprint of Simon & Schuster Children's Publishing Division
1230 Avenue of the Americas, New York, NY 10020
First Aladdin paperback edition July 2014
Text copyright © 1960 by Marguerite Henry
Cover illustrations copyright © 2014 by John Rowe
Interior illustrations copyright © 1960 by Lynd Ward
All rights reserved, including the right of reproduction in whole or in part in any form.
ALADDIN is a trademark of Simon & Schuster, Inc., and related logo is a registered trademark of Simon & Schuster, Inc.
For information about special discounts for bulk purchases, please contact Simon & Schuster Special Sales at 1-866-506-1949 or business@simonandschuster.com.
Cover designed by Jeanine Henderson
The text of this book was set in Adobe Garamond Pro.
Manufactured in the United States of America 0614 OFF
10 9 8 7 6 5 4 3 2 1
Library of Congress Control Number 2014938916
ISBN 978-1-4814-0397-9
ISBN 978-1-4814-0399-3 (eBook)

*To the half-bred Arabian, Gaudenzia,*
*and to her boy trainer, Giorgio,*
*who lived this book with*
*honor and valor*

# Contents

## FOREWORD

For months I wrote the story of the Palio in my mind. I pictured a fearless boy rider in this wildest of all horse races, a boy who dared defy the ancient rules and *willed* his horse to win—in spite of the strict orders of his captain.

When I finally went to Siena and faced the real battle of the Palio, I had to scuttle my preconceived plot. No rider, no matter how brave, would ever defy the ancient rules of the race. They are as firm and immutable as the walls of the city.

But the story I found was of heroic proportions, much bigger than the one I had dreamed. A peasant boy, named Giorgio Terni, and a half-bred Arabian mare seemed pawns of fate, doomed to a life of tragedy. Their battle to outwit destiny is a drama of human and animal courage.

The secret plotting of the Palio is so strange that I had to journey from America to Siena three times in order to understand the inner workings. There is a need in the people to relive the past, a need so intense that they change themselves into knights and noblemen of the Middle Ages for a brief moment each year.

While I was there, I myself became embroiled in the passion of the Palio. I attended the solemn ritualistic banquet on the eve of the race, and afterward I went with Giorgio Terni and his bodyguards to listen to music in the heart of the Piazza, and I went with him into the stable of the mare, Gaudenzia. I wanted to study this courageous youth who was fully aware that tomorrow his blood and that of his mount might crimson the race course.

I visited with Giorgio's parents, too, and with his brother and sister in the huddled village of Monticello, far away in the Maremma country. Because I spoke no Italian we had to communicate in pantomime, but it was more exciting than any game of charades. It concerned life, and death.

Twice I watched spellbound the pageant-parade on Palio day, and twice I shouted and prayed during the breakneck race that Gaudenzia would sweep wildly through the pack to victory.

Dozens of people—cobblers and captains, peasants and princes—gave of their time and energy to help make this book an authentic recreation of the oldest horse race in the long history of the sport of kings.

At last I understood that the Palio is a fire banked but never quenched. Every summer it blazes anew into a festival of such drama and color that the characters who take part might have stepped out of the Middle Ages.

MARGUERITE HENRY

# GAUDENZIA, PRIDE OF THE PALIO

*Chapter I*

THE FIRST SIGNPOST

In a hill town of Italy, close by the Tyrrhenian Sea, lives the boy, Giorgio Terni. He is slight of build but hard-muscled and lithe, with dark wavy hair and amber eyes the color of a young fox's. His town, Monticello Amiata, is named for nearby Mount Amiata. But the countryside that dips down to the sea is known as the Maremma, or "marshy place." It was once wild and desolate, and it bred strong, earthy men who grappled their living from the wetlands.

In the rest of Italy people still think of the Maremma

as a savage, wind-blown place where land and sea are not yet separated. They have heard that only work horses and bullocks are reared there, and the people who survive the fever-laden mosquitoes are wild as the sea that goes to meet the sky.

But now things are changing. The bogs and sea ponds are being ditched and drained, and the tangle of brown swamp grass is giving way to fields of golden wheat, and to olive groves and vineyards.

Giorgio's father is one of the new farmers. He cultivates a narrow strip of land, and at harvest time pays a little money to the state so that in twenty or thirty years it will be his. But at heart the new farmers remain unchanged. The love of animals is strong in their blood, and they tell with pride that the horses of the Maremma stand taller and show more stamina than those bred elsewhere.

It was in Giorgio's thirteenth year that he resolved to make animals his life. Two experiences came to him in swift succession—one brutal, one tantalizing. When he thought about them later, he knew they were signposts, pointing the way to his future.

Work-hardened and tough as he was, the first one shook him like a thunderbolt. He was driving Pippa, his donkey, from the hilltop village of Monticello down to the valley of his father's farmland. It was a clear, bright day, with only a capful of wind. Spring was in the air—grapevines sending out new runners, swallows hunting straws.

Then all at once the bright morning went black with horror. Near a wayside shrine Giorgio came upon a swineherd mercilessly beating a small, shaggy donkey. With each blow the dust rose in little clouds from the donkey's back. As Giorgio drove up, he saw that the creature was trying to lunge away, but he was tied fast to a tree. The sight threw the boy into a blinding rage. He jumped from the cart and caught at the rope.

"Stop it!" he shouted to the swineherd. "You'll kill him!"

The man turned in surprise, sweat dripping from the beardy stubble on his chin. He jerked the rope from Giorgio's hand. "Why not kill him?" he bawled out. "Too stubborn he is to live!" Taking a fresh hold on the stick, he hit the donkey across the rump, the back, the ears.

"Stop!" Giorgio shouted again. He braced his feet. His arm muscles went hard and tight. He waited for the stick to crack across his face. But it did not come. It kept right on flogging the mouse-colored donkey, *a-whack, a-whing,* and *a-whack,* until with a grunt more sob than bray, he fell to his knees.

Giorgio crouched over the poor beast and stroked his head. Nearby he saw two crates filled with squealing pigs. He gave the swineherd a scornful look. "Let *me* load your donkey," he cried. "Let *me* drive him to market."

With one arm the man flung the boy out of his path, then came stalking at him, making bull's horns of his first and fourth fingers. He thrust them almost into Giorgio's eyes. "You meddling runt! How'd you like the stick against *your* hide! Run for your life, or I . . ." His hand came up in a threat.

Giorgio stood his ground. He was only a little afraid. He hated the smell of the sweat-dripping man.

Something in the boy's face made the man change his mind. He threw the stick far off into the field. "All right, you runt!" He spat the words between his yellowed teeth. "You so smart, *you* load Long-ears! *You* drive my shoats to market."

"I will! But first I drive Pippa to our farm." The boy ran back to his cart, lifted Pippa's head with the lines, and down the road the donkey clippety-clopped as if there were no time to lose. Giorgio glanced back to make sure the swineherd would wait. The man had flopped down in a slab of shade made by the shrine. He was mopping his face and at the same time pulling a plug of tobacco from his pocket.

The farm was only a kilometer away, and Giorgio soon returned on foot. With tiny new carrots and a pocketful of grain, he coaxed the donkey to his feet. Carefully he loaded him with the crates of pigs, making sure the ropes did not bind, and he tucked rags under the pack to cushion the weight against the sores. Then slowly he led the donkey to market, talking and praising him all the way. The swineherd, sullen and silent, plod-ded along behind.

Three times that week Giorgio worked Long-ears, and he neither kicked nor balked. He seemed to know a friend was leading him. He accepted each load meekly, as if it were the sun or the rain. He even let himself be ridden, the boy sitting far back between the crates singing "*Fu-ni-cu-li! Fu-ni-cu-la!*" at the top of his lungs.

The market men poked fun at the swineherd. "Giorgio, he makes cuckoo of you!" they laughed in his face. "Long-ears is fine worker, for the boy."

The taunts enraged the man, and when no one was looking, he continued to take out his fury on the donkey. There came a morning when the little beast no longer felt the pain of the floggings. He was dead.

When the news reached Giorgio, he stopped what he was doing and made a hard fist of his right hand. Then he struck the palm of his other hand again and again, until the stinging made him quit. The hurt somehow helped him feel better, as if he had delivered the blows to the swineherd's fat, dripping face.

On the surface, life went on as before. Giorgio worked in the fields with his father and his younger brother, Emilio. And he worked for his mother and his sister, fetching water in great copper pitchers from the street fountain, and carrying trays of neatly shaped dough to the public bake oven. But he thought often of the swineherd's cruelty.

One noontime when he and his father had stopped their span of white bullocks, he spoke in great seriousness. *"Babbo,"* he asked, "you will not laugh if I tell you what I will do when I have a few more years?"

"I will not laugh," the father replied as he opened Giorgio's schoolbag that now served as lunchbag.

"You promise it?"

"I promise."

The boy accepted the hunk of bread and the wild boar sausage the father offered. Then his arm made a great arc toward the mountains. "Some day," he said in a hushed tone, "I will be a trainer of animals, not just donkeys. And I will climb Mount Amiata and live in the land on the other side."

The father nodded as he chewed. Young boys' heads

were full of dreams. He had once dreamed of leaving the Maremma country himself. "It costs dear to travel," he warned.

"That I know, Babbo, but I will have my own horse and he will take me." Giorgio's imagination was on fire. "Everyone will try to buy him. For me he will walk forward or backward, trot or gallop, or spin around in a circle. All this he will do—not in fear, but because he wants to please me."

"For you, my son, I hope all comes true. But do you forget that times are hard and your Babbo has to sell horseflesh for eating, not riding?"

Giorgio was only half listening; he was on a big-going horse, sailing right over the cone of Mount Amiata.

If the swineherd and his donkey had planted a seed in Giorgio's mind, it was the Umbrella Man who made it grow. He came yodeling into Monticello one misting morning three months later.

"*Om-brel-lai-o-o-o!*" His voice rang out strong and clear as the bell in the church tower. "*Om-brel-lai-o-o-o!* I doctor the broken ribs! I patch and mend! Pots and pans, and china, too. *Om-brel-lai-o-o-o!*" And he strung out the word until it rolled and bounced from house to house.

Shutters flew open, heads popped out of windows. A crock of geraniums fell with a crash on the cobblestones below. Children danced for joy, old men brandished their canes like batons. Giorgio, who had been filling pitchers at the public fountain, ran for home, spilling the water as he flew.

"*Mammina!*" he cried as he burst into the kitchen. "He is here! Uncle Marco, the Umbrella Man!"

His mother turned away from the stove, smiling. It was good for a change to have Giorgio seem more boy than man. She took from the opposite wall, next to the family's hats and caps, an enormous green umbrella with a loose hanging fold made by a broken rib. "The tinker man works magic if he can fix this," she laughed.

In a flash Giorgio was at the door, umbrella in hand.

"Wait, son! Wait!" She looked at the eager boy and quickly counted in her mind the pieces of money in the sugar pot—the soldi and the lire. Yes, if she carried the big red hen and one or two rabbits to market, there would again be the same money in the pot.

She went to the end of the narrow room that served as kitchen, dining, and living room. Opening the bottom doors of a tall cupboard, she took out the broken pieces of a bake dish. It was the one, Giorgio saw, that he had clumsily dropped on the stone floor. Next she counted out a hundred lire.

"Now then," she said, putting the money and the broken dish into his hands, "go quickly. With the umbrella *and* the bake dish to mend, you can ask more questions than anyone who brings just the umbrella. You are happy, no?"

Thinking of the cost, Giorgio looked at his mother in astonishment. Ever since the incident of the donkey she had tried in little ways to make up for his sorrow. She had fried crispy hot *fritelle* for him when it wasn't even a feast day. And only last night he had found under his pillow the last piece of nougat left from Christmas. Now this joy! For it was Uncle Marco's rule that whoever brought him the most work could ask the most questions.

"*Si! Si!*" he answered, kissing her soundly on the cheek. Then he threw back his head, and whinnying like a King Horse ran joyously out of the house.

*Chapter II*

THE UMBRELLA MAN

On the edge of the public fountain, where three narrow lanes come together, the Umbrella Man sat perched like some Robin Hood alighted only for the moment. He wore a brimmed hat with the tail feathers of a cock pheasant stuck through the felt. His shoes were brown leather curled upward at the toes, and the soles were of wood, rubbed shiny. When he lifted his arms one could tell that his jacket had once been bright green. Now it was powdered by dust—not gray dust, not brown, but tawny red—testimony to long days of walking the hills of Tuscany.

Yet with all his traveling the Umbrella Man showed no sign of weariness. His eyes, dark and beady, sparkled in delight, as if this were a day he had long awaited, as if it held a special quality, rare and magical.

*"Buon giorno! Buon giorno!"* He opened wide his arms to welcome his friends who came laughing and breathless to greet him. One other boy brought a sagging umbrella, and a girl carried a pitcher with a broken snout. They, with Giorgio, placed their crippled possessions at his feet, like precious offerings laid before a god.

Before starting to work, Uncle Marco looked from face to face, beaming. He was actor as well as tinker. He had certain little curtain-raiser habits to whet the excitement. First he made a ritual of taking off his hat, running his fingers over the bright glinting feathers, and putting it back on again at a rakish angle. Then while his audience watched in growing impatience, he took a copper mug from his pocket, and let the fountain water flow into it. He drank long and heartily, sucking the water through his ragged red whiskers with a loud hissing sound.

*"Bello! Bello!"* he sang out. "No water so delicious as water of Monticello!" His voice rolled strong and vibrant, full of the juices of living. *"Bello, bello—Monticello!"* he sang again, clapping his hands, chuckling over his rhyme.

At last, with a grand flourish, he unhooked the pack on his back and spread out its contents on the cobblestones.

The children craned their necks to see umbrella ribs made of canewood, patches of green and black and purple cloth, rolls of thin wire, an old fish tin, a needle curved like a serpent's tongue, and a wondrous drill that looked for all the world like a bow and arrow. With a jovial wink in Giorgio's direction, the Umbrella Man now took up the broken bake dish.

"Giorgio Terni!" he pronounced in his best stage voice. "With you we begin. Of the world beyond the mountain, what is it you want to know? Ask, boy."

Giorgio's heart beat wildly. He swallowed; he gulped. Emilio, his little brother, and Teria, his sister, crowded in on him, nudging him with their elbows. "Ask it!" they urged. "Ask!"

Giorgio knew what to ask, but he muffled and stammered the words so they ran all together. "YoujustcomefromSiena?" he whispered.

"Eh? Speak out. Speak out, boy! *Forte!*"

"You just come from over the mountain? From city of Siena?" This time the question could be heard by everyone, even by people leaning out the windows.

The pheasant feathers danced and nodded a vigorous "yes," and the twinkling black eyes looked up, encouraging the next question.

"You see the big horse race? The *Palio?*"

"I see it, all right. I see both July *and* August Palio!"
Everyone pressed close, heads canted, listening.

A spotted pig wandered into the crowd, snuffling and snorting, but went unnoticed. All eyes were fixed on the Umbrella Man, watching fascinated, as slowly, deliberately, he worked on the bake dish. First he loosened the bowstring of the drill. Then he sawed away clockwise, then counterclockwise, making the tip of the arrow drill a neat little hole in the dish.

Impatience mounted while he drilled three more holes and inspected each one carefully, nodding in approval.

"We wire and glue later. Now then," he sighed, with a glance to the far-off hills. "Now I carry everyone over the mountain to old, walled city of Siena!" He opened up the big green umbrella as if they could all hang onto the spokes and fly away together.

"The Palio," he began, taking a deep breath, "is fierce battle *and* race all at same time. If I tell you, you must listen. Even if it makes the hairs on your spine to quiver. Even if you do not believe it can be so!"

The fountain place was so still that the drip-drip from the spigot sounded like hammer strokes.

"Anciently," he went on, "in old, old times before anyone remembers, city of Siena was very powerful nation."

Giorgio nodded to himself. This was going to be good. Not a tall tale but a true one.

"Inside her high old walls she is divided like inside

this umbrella. Only instead of cloth and ribs, she is divided sharp and clean into districts called *contradas.*"

Giorgio opened his mouth. "Do they have names?"

"Oh, splendid names—mostly for animals. One contrada is the Dragon, another the Panther, the Eagle, the Porcupine, the Wolf, the Owl. Like that," he said, ticking them off on his nimble fingers. "Seventeen they number in all."

The pig came back, stole a piece of apple from a child's fingers, and scampered away again. But the child did not even whimper. There was just the Umbrella Man, his eyes hypnotic, his voice carrying his audience along, farther and farther from Monticello.

"In Middle Ages, each contrada was great military company of knights in armor, and each had beautiful flag with emblem in gold. And they fought blood wars."

Suddenly the Umbrella Man's face beaded in sweat. His skin paled.

"Uncle Marco! What is it?" an elderly man asked anxiously. "Are you sick?"

"No, no." He narrowed his eyes and leaned forward. "How can I explain how fierce, how strong, how loyal are feelings in each contrada even to this day?" He shook his head in despair. "Just for suppose: A father belongs to the Contrada of the Panther, the mother to the Dragon, one son to the Eagle, the other to the Ram. You see, it's where you're born that makes you Eagle or Ram or Panther or Dragon."

He stopped to blot the perspiration with a bright red handkerchief.

"How do I explain? All year long this family lives together in happy feelings. Then come the preparations for the Palio, and—*pffft!*—they are enemies! In the father the Panther blood runs like fever. He forgets home; he goes to the meetings. Every afternoon, every night, in every spare time he joins the other Panthers. They make questions. 'Who will be our jockey in the Palio race?' 'Shall we make the alliances with other contradas?' 'Who shall paint with gold the hoofs of our horse if we win?' 'Who shall be in charge of our Victory Dinner?'

"And Mamma? She is not like Mamma at all. She lets the spaghetti burn. She snips and sews all day for the Dragon—mending their silken banners and the velvet costumes for the parade.

"Mind you," Uncle Marco shook his forefinger wildly, "some costumes were designed by Leonardo da Vinci! No wonder the Mamma's hands tremble while she works . . . so great the honor is!"

Giorgio interrupted. "Uncle Marco! What about the two brothers?"

"Well, those boys, they grow warlike against each other and their father must separate them; he sends them to stay with friends or cousins in their special contradas."

"For both Palios?"

"For both!" The man shrugged helplessly. "Who can

understand this mystic feeling—mad, wonderful?" He waved his hand in staccato rhythm. "It is war! It is history! It is religion! All year long the Palio is a fire banked. Then it stirs; it blazes; it comes like flames sweeping down the centuries. Oh, how beautiful the faces light up and the voices sing and the banners wave!" He closed his eyes to see it all the better, and the quiet was like an intermission, only no one stirred.

Giorgio waited in a torment of suspense until at last he had to break through. "But Uncle Marco! Speak of the race! *Please!*"

The man shook off his trance. "I enter into that now." He shivered in excitement. "First comes the story parade. Is it a common parade?" he bellowed to his rapt audience.

"No!" they roared in reply.

With an elfish chuckle, he clapped his hands approvingly. "Siena," he sucked in a long breath, "lives upon remembrance of her ancient glory. Each year, for seven hundred years, she is celebrating the Victory of Montaperti. Even the gold battle car is there in the parade. And the people watch in awe, remembering their blood is the blood of their fathers shed to win that battle."

"But the race! The race!" Giorgio insisted.

"All right! All right! When the parade is over, a bomb explodes *bang!* And out come the horses wearing the bright colors of their contradas. Away they go like quiver of arrows shot all at once. Around the town square—one time, two times, three times! And the *fantinos* who ride them sit bareback. They cling like the monkey. They risk life. Heads broken. Shoulders. Legs. Arms. Only the brave . . ."

"Uncle Marco!" cried Giorgio. "Must the fantinos belong to a contrada?"

"No, no! They are outsiders, from beyond the city walls. But listen!" He lowered his voice to a whisper. "That race course is death trap. Up, down, up, down, and around sharp curves. Dizzy-high buildings come so close they bump the horses, almost.

"But now comes the best part!" His voice rose in power and excitement. "If the fantino falls off, the horse can win all by himself—*if* . . ."

"If what?" the children cried.

"If no one has knocked off his *spennacchiera*."

The children's eyes popped. "His *what*?"

Uncle Marco pushed back his hat and held three fingers upright against his forehead. "This is my spen-nac-chie-ra," and he spun out the syllables until they seemed to have springs in them. "You see, my friends, it is like colored plumes in the headband of each horse. It is the badge of his contrada."

With his free hand he now picked up an umbrella rib. "This is my *nerbo*," he explained. "It is fierce whip of ox hide, used always by fantinos since olden years." In make-believe anger he used it to whack his fingers away from his forehead.

24

Emilio and the younger children all made imaginary plumes of their fingers and some tried to knock off their neighbor's until the audience was in a shrieking uproar.

While Uncle Marco waited for quiet, he went to work on the green umbrella, snipped out the offending rib, and with the long, curved needle sewed a new one in place.

Giorgio watched with unseeing eyes. He was still far away in Siena. When the noise died down he said, "Uncle Marco, the contrada that wins, what does it win?"

"What does it win! Why, it wins the *Palio,* the silken banner!"

"Only a banner?"

The needle went in and out, fast and faster, and the man's face darkened in displeasure. "*Only* a banner! How can you say it? The picture of the Madonna is hand-painted on it! Why, the winning of the banner is like . . ." He rummaged around in his mind for something big enough . . . "is like finding the Holy Grail."

"Oh." Giorgio's face went red. He lowered his head in embarrassment.

The time for asking questions was nearly up. The Umbrella Man was mixing cement in the old fish tin, gluing the broken dish together, fastening it through the drilled holes with fine wire. While his fingers worked, his eye stole a glance now and then at Giorgio.

"Maybe some year you go to Siena? You see a Palio?"

Giorgio's head jerked up. Of course he would go!

Then his eyes widened in sudden panic. Suppose the race stopped before he had saved enough money. Suppose next year, or the next, there should be no Palio!

He spoke his fears aloud.

"Ho! Ho!" The Umbrella Man rocked with laughter. "Palio has always been! That is fine reason why it always will be. You go *any* year. Time only sharpens the appetite."

At sundown that evening, with the mended dish put away in the cupboard and the umbrella, good as new, hanging on its peg, Giorgio stood before the window at the end of the long room. It was flung wide to the hills of Tuscany, but the boy did not see the trees flaming from the touch of sun, nor the swallows tumbling in the sky, nor the mountains growing bluer with the oncoming night. All he saw was the clay model of the horse in his hands. As he pinched and shaped the legs to a breedy fineness, a piece of leftover clay fell to the floor. He picked it up, examining it in disbelief. Did he imagine, or could *anyone* see it for what it was?

"Emilio! Teria!" he called. "Come here! Come and see!"

He held up the fanlike piece of clay, the smaller end between his thumb and forefinger, and he moved it toward the head of the horse. "What is it?" he asked, scarcely daring to breathe.

"Why, it's a spen-nac-chie-ra!" the answer came in chorus. "A spen-nac-chie-ra!"

Giorgio laughed out loud. He moistened his finger tips and firmly pressed the bit of clay on the poll of the horse's head. "Let no fantino knock it off!" he spoke to the little image. "You win all by yourself, you hear?"

Already the seed of the Palio was bursting in its furrow.

*Chapter III*

BIANCA, THE BLIND ONE

After the Umbrella Man left, there was a sense of urgency in the way Giorgio lived and worked. If he was to become a fantino in the Palio, or a horse trainer, or only a groom, he must grow hard, wiry, quick; and stronger than boys twice his size.

His mother and father could not understand the change in their eldest. Instead of turning over for an extra sleep in the morning, he was up before the sun—feeding the cats in the kitchen, clanking the copper pitchers as he went to fetch the drinking water, graining Pippa, mending harness.

And when the cocks had only begun to crow, he was already at the door with the donkey hitched to the cart. Together he and his father went whistling off into the morning.

It was only nine kilometers to their farm, but the road wound down through stern country. Pippa was trail-wise. Where the footing was good she went trotting along, ears flopping, tail swinging; but through the tangled brake where the wild boar lurked, she kept her head down, watchful, snuffing. Of the few hovels they passed she always remembered the one where the swineherd and his poor donkey had lived; there she slowed her steps and gave out a sad, wheezy bray. Giorgio's whistling stopped, for he remembered, too. Then he looked away, looked at the great dark hulk of Mount Amiata, and knew that on the other side the morning sun was warming the foothills and somewhere there in the brightness was the ancient, walled city of Siena. The very name made his hairs stir. It was like a finger beckoning to him, urging him to hurry in his growing.

He always sat up straight then and called out, "Pippa! Get along! We go to work."

Plash! Plash! Pippa's feet plunged through the ditch at the edge of their farm, clambered up the other side, and headed for the barn.

To Giorgio, his whole life seemed wrapped up in the big barn made of bricks and straw. Here were the horses his father bought and sold—sometimes five, sometimes seven—and here were the team of white bullocks, and the milk-cow, and a frisky goat and her twin kids. With a sad sort of smile Babbo each morning encouraged Giorgio to grain the horses well, for the more fat on their bones the better price they would bring.

There was one mare, however, that Giorgio fed meagerly, for he loved her most and wanted no one to buy her. She was steel-gray with lively ears and enormous eyes, but they were blind. He felt guilty in his heart when he grained the others; it was like sending them to their death. But he felt guiltier still when he gave only small measure to Bianca, the blind one. Her ribs showed when he cleaned her off, and when he rode her, his legs could feel each one separately. He took to sitting well forward to ease his conscience. Then he was scarcely any weight at all.

To make up for the scanty meals, he often brought her fistfuls of clover. And in her stall the straw bedding was always the deepest.

One day Giorgio's father, pointing to Bianca, said, "That one is a terrible sorrow to me. It is not enough she is blind and unable to work. But besides, she does not fatten."

"Give her time, Babbo."

"Time! Already dozens of horses come and go, but Bianca, she stays. And only from pity I took her. I say to myself, 'We give her two, three weeks of good eating; then we let her go.'" The father shook his head, frowning. "A blind mare, she is good for nothing."

"Maybe," Giorgio ventured, "she could make a good colt."

"No, no. Her colts, too, could come blind. And she is not good for the riding, either."

"Oh, but she is! She is more sure-footed than . . ." Giorgio suddenly broke off his praise. If anyone knew how big-going she was and how willing and trustful, she would be sold in a hurry to some traveler, or even as a race horse. Then he would never see her again. Never ride her again. Never feel her lips nuzzling his neck to make sure that he was *he*! "Yes," he nodded in agreement, "it is too bad about the blind one." And he became very busy, mucking out her stall to hide his blushing.

Giorgio's tasks were endless. With the bullock team he plowed and cultivated the cornfield. By hand he hoed the beans and peas. He milked the cow. He kept the rabbit hutch clean. He staked out the she-goat by day and brought her in at night.

But these seemed mere child's tasks. He liked better to swing the scythe in harvest time. Cutting down the sun-ripened hay was man's work. He could feel his muscles hardening, his lungs swelling. He took a fierce pride in piling the hay around a pole, piling it higher and higher until it was ready for the thatched roof that became the watershed.

If he tired toward the end of the day, he made himself remember the mocking grin of the swineherd and the voice sneering, "You meddling runt, you!" The memory gave him a new burst of strength. He gripped the scythe like one possessed of a demon, and he cut the hay in great wide swaths.

He felt better then, and to reward himself for the extra work he went around to the barn, bridled Bianca, and rode pell-mell into the gathering dusk. It was good to let the wind wash his face, to let the smooth, rocking motion ease his body. He could ride for miles through weeds and grasses without crossing a road, and he exulted in the fearlessness with which Bianca faced the unknown.

Heading back to the stable one night, Giorgio let his bare legs dangle along the mare's sides, and to his surprise he could not feel her ribs.

"Babbo!" he exclaimed when he brought her in. "Bianca is shaping up! But please . . ."

The father interrupted. "I know, I know, and it is costing dear. Since you grain her night and morning, I grain her extra at noon. A heaping measure I give her, with sugar added."

Giorgio looked up in fear. "Please, Babbo, please don't sell her. I pretend always she is mine. With her, the eyes are not needed. She's *got* eyes—in her ears, in her feet, in her heart. Babbo, don't sell her."

There was a mark of pain between the father's eyes. "Son," he said, "she goes sure-footed only with you. With the others she stumbles. Her owner before us told me she breaks a man's leg in falling on him. Giorgio, I got nothing to say. Families come first. Emilio and Teria and Mamma got to eat."

Two mornings later the blind mare's stall was empty. Giorgio felt himself too old to cry. He found some of her tail hairs caught in the wood of the manger, and very gently he pulled them out, as if they were still a part of her. He braided them and put them as a keepsake in the back of the big watch his grandfather had left him.

It was not until he arrived in Monticello that evening and his mother said, "Giorgio, maybe somebody today hurt you?" that he wept. The room was empty. Emilio and Teria had gone to their cousins' for supper and the father was unhooking Pippa. Now, alone with his mother, the boy's pent-up feelings burst.

She put her mending aside and with a quiet hand on his shoulder said, "I think I know. It is Bianca who is gone this time. Your father, too, is troubled. All night long he can't sleep."

Giorgio did not ask the fate of the blind mare. He knew. But in his sorrow he clung to a frail thread of comfort. After his voice steadied he asked, "When a creature goes to die, do you believe . . ." The words came strained, begging for help, trying to find a way to ask it. "That is, do you think a newborn comes to take the place of the other?"

The mother understood the boy's need. Slowly, thoughtfully, she said, "This I have pondered also." Then a look of triumph lighted her face, as if two things suddenly fitted together. "Si!" she said with conviction, "when one leaves this life, another *must* come into it. Yesterday," she went on, "when I was washing our bed linen at the public washbasins, a farmer from Magliano Toscano galloped by." She drove her needle in and out of a button already sewn fast. "He was followed by a veterinarian on a second beast. They were in a very great hurry. You see," she added with a quick catch of her breath, "the farmer's mare had been bred to the Arabian stallion, Sans Souci, and she was due to foal. Her colt, of course, would be of royal blood!"

"Well, *did she?*"

The mother's hand made the sign of the cross. Then she looked happily at Giorgio and her voice was full of assurance. "She did! The news today carried all the way to our marketplace. Her colt, Giorgio, is a filly. And she has the eyes to see!"

## Chapter IV

### A NEWBORN

The daughter of Sans Souci was already foaled when the farmer and the horse doctor arrived in Magliano Toscano. She was already dropped on the bed of straw, and there she lay, flat and wet, like a rug left out in the rain. Her eyes were closed and her nostrils not even fluttering.

The doctor, a sharp-eyed, determined little man, hastily pulled out his stethoscope, and falling to his knees in the straw, held it to the foal's side, listening. The farmer stood looking on, pale and helpless. No less a person than Sans Souci's owner, the Prince of Lombardy, wanted to buy the foal, but only if it were sound and sturdy. He had even agreed to pay the horse doctor's fee. Would he, if she died? She must not die!

"The heart?" the farmer whispered anxiously. "It beats? No?"

"Only faint," the doctor replied, "like butterfly wings." Straightening up, he snapped out his orders. "You got to help. Lift her up! No! No! Not like that. By her hind legs, hang her upside down. The blood, it's *got* to flow to the brain."

Frightened into submission, the farmer did as he was told while the doctor began furiously rubbing the foal's sides. The perfect little head was thrust back, mouth agape. The doctor stopped a moment, placed his hands against her chest, but there were still no signs of breathing. He pulled an old towel from his satchel, doused it in the watering trough, and slapped the colt. "Wake up!" he cried. "Get courage, little one! Breathe! Ahead lies the world!"

Still no response. The gray lump hung from the farmer's hands like a carcass in a butcher shop.

"What we do now?" the farmer asked.

"Lay her down!" the doctor shouted, unwilling to give up. "Fetch the wheelbarrow."

Puzzled, the farmer hurried out to the lean-to beside the barn.

The doctor crouched on his knees and with slow,

forceful motions pressed the tiny squeeze-box of the colt's ribs. "Breathe! Breathe! Breathe!" he panted as he tried to pump air into her lungs.

The mare all this while had been lying exhausted. She lifted her head now and let out a cry that was half squeal, half whinny. As if in answer, there was a gasp from her foal. Then a shallow cough, followed by a whimper.

When the farmer came rattling in with the wheelbarrow, he stopped in awe. "She does not go under!" he exclaimed. Then he laughed in relief. "The wheelbarrow—you don't need now?"

"Now I do!" Cheeks flushed in triumph, the doctor kept on pumping air into the filly's lungs and at the same time barking out directions: "Be quick! Fill a gunny sack with straw! Lay it flat on the wheelbarrow!"

The gasps were coming closer together. They were stronger. And stronger.

The doctor stopped pumping. He listened through his stethoscope and heaved a deep sigh. "Is greatest thing I ever see! The mare, she helped me just in time." Proudly, he lifted the newborn on top of the stuffed gunny sack. "We take her now into your kitchen and dry her by your fire."

"But why?" the farmer asked, more puzzled than before. "Why, when already she breathes?"

"Please to remember this, my friend. For eleven months she is living in a very warm place. Today is windly, and it blows cool into the barn."

Nodding, the farmer trundled the little creature past the stalls of cows and bullocks and through the door that led into the kitchen.

"Maria!" he called to his wife as he lifted the foal from the wheelbarrow and placed her beside the fire. "See what it is we bring!"

The farmer's wife, a plump, pleasant woman with eyes as shiny as olives, came running from another room. Politely she greeted the doctor, set out a bottle of her best wine and a glass on the table for him. Then in an instant she was on her knees cooing, "Ah, poor little one, poor dear one!" Without thinking, she had taken off her homespun apron and was rubbing the filly as if its ribs were a washboard.

*"Brava! Brava!"* cried the doctor between sips of the golden wine. "Your wife," he remarked to the farmer, "is a nurse most competent. Guard well you do not burn the little one so close to the fire. Rub the legs and the body until nice and dry. Then take her back to her dam." He knelt down and put a finger in the filly's mouth. "See? Already she sucks! By herself she will find the mare's milk faucets. And now I must leave. *Arrivederci,* my good people."

The doctor's happy laughter rang out behind him as he walked across the dooryard to the hitching post.

In the warm kitchen a second miracle was taking place. The foal, yawning, looking about with her purple-brown eyes, was stretching her forelegs, learning so soon that legs were for standing!

The farmer slowly shook his head as if now he saw her for the first time, her frailty, her pipestem legs.

"Already I have a name for her," he said dully.

"So? How will you call her?"

"*Farfalla*. Butterfly."

"Is so beautiful," Maria sighed.

"Beauty, bah! Is not enough." In the farmer's eyes was a look almost of hatred. "A *stout* horse the Prince of Lombardy wanted. Nice strong legs to race over the cobble streets of Siena. With a colt by Sans Souci he hoped to win a Palio. Better that horse doctor never came!"

With a flirt of her tail, the foal tried a step, and fell down in a fuzzy heap.

The farmer winced, almost as if he heard a leg snap and break. "Spindle legs have no place in Palio," he snorted. "And for sure I cannot use such a skinny beast in farm work. Better the hand of death had taken her. Farfalla," he laughed bitterly. "She will live only the short and useless life of the butterfly."

The Prince of Lombardy did not come to see the colt for several days. He was a busy man—an art collector and a sportsman who raced his horses not only in Italy but in France and Spain. His burning desire, however, was to win a Palio. This, he knew, required a special kind of horse, one not too finely wrought.

He knew too that the marshy land of the Maremma made an excellent breeding ground, developing horses with strong, heavy bone. And so he let the farmers of the Maremma bring their mares to his Arabian stallion to be bred. Then if the mating brought forth a strong, rugged colt, he would agree to buy it at weaning time.

When he finally arrived at Magliano Toscano late one afternoon, the farmer broke into a nervous sweat. Maybe, he thought to himself, the Prince will buy the little one, not for the Palio but for racing on dirt tracks.

The mare and colt were out in a field at the time, wallowing in a sea of grass. The farmer whistled them in, and as they approached, he turned to the Prince. "Here comes Farfalla!" He trumpeted the words as if they could make the filly as big as the shout. "She will lighten in color, Signore, and become pure white, like Sans Souci. No?"

A quizzical expression crossed the Prince's face. He watched the foal dance and curvet in front of him. His eyes went over her, inch by inch, studying her legs, her hindquarters. After a seeming eternity, he repeated her name. "Farfalla," he mused. "The name suits her well. She appears capricious, nervous; not what I had hoped. She has none of the bulk and brawn of the dam. But nonetheless I will pay the cost of the veterinarian, and it is my hope you will find some use for her."

Waving his gauntlets in good-bye, he stepped into his open-top car and roared off into the twilight.

*Chapter V*

## THE FLYING CENTAUR

The filly grew—skittish and frivolous as her name. Every time the farmer let her out of her stall she bolted past him, and snorting like a steam engine, she flew down the aisle, sending goats and geese scuttling out of her way. Then at the end stall she slowed just long enough to sink her teeth into the buttocks of the black bullock. In the split second before he could kick back, she was out in the sunlight, squeaking a high hello to the world.

"It is a painful thing for the bullock," the farmer told

his wife one day. "But if he is not there, the rascal nips me in the pants instead."

The wife burst into a fit of laughter. She threw her apron over her face to stifle her merriment.

"Bah!" the farmer stormed. "Women and fillies, they think alike! For them biting is a funny joke." And he stomped out of the kitchen, slamming the door behind him.

Away in Monticello, young Giorgio Terni inquired of travelers and tradesmen about the daughter of Sans Souci. He learned only that she was fiery and mischievous, unlike her work-horse mother. But he dreamed often that she had taken the place of his blind mare. In his dreaming she was an Arabian all the way—an Arabian whose ancestors had raced swiftly across the sun-scorched desert. She would be steel-gray, of course, with her muzzle nearly black, and her fine legs black from knees and hocks to hoof, and her eyes enormous and dark. As for size, he thought of her as big enough.

He longed to see her, but Magliano Toscano was many kilometers away, and now was the season of the grape harvest.

Each morning before daybreak, the whole family piled into the donkey cart and drove off to their vineyard. Up and down the rows they snipped the purple bunches, dew-drenched in the morning, shiny warm in the glare of noon. They filled basket after basket to roundness, and emptied them into big tubs. It was Giorgio who lugged them, two at a time, to the wine shed, dumping the grapes, stems and all, into a huge vat. Then at dusk after the animals had been fed, he clambered up the wall of the vat, grasped the pole across the open top, swung himself inside, and with his bare feet pushed down the slippery seeds and skins that had risen to the surface.

One evening when the family, dusty and weary, was returning home by starlight, Giorgio spoke shyly to his mother. "Some day I would go to Magliano to see the filly of Sans Souci . . . if only I had the time."

"Maybe on Sunday after the mass," the mother suggested.

"I will go!" he cried, and the weariness of the long day suddenly melted.

But Giorgio did not go. On the next Sunday he was chosen watchkeeper of the church. And now the Sundays stretched out longer than all the other days. He had to scrub the floor inside the church and sweep the earth outside. He had to dust the altars. He had to arrange the benches and chairs. He had to play the bells, calling the people from houses and barns. He had to help serve mass. And when the services were over, he remained on watch. Alone in the deep hush, he listened to the wind moaning in the cypress trees, reminding him that each tree in the churchyard stood for a soldier dead. He tried to close his ears to the dismal sound, but the trees kept on whispering, and the mourning doves added their plaintive lament.

There was reward, however, in being watchkeeper. It meant that the people of Monticello considered him more man than boy. His voice was changing, too, and now when he sang in the choir it cracked, sliding far off key.

"Tsk, tsk!" the father remarked one Sunday. "Our Giorgio is getting a voice most strange. More howl than human. Sometimes," he laughed, "I look up quick to see, is he growing flap ears like basset hound, or great furred ones, like Pippa? Because he knows how animals think, must he sing like them, too?"

The family was seated around the table eating their Sunday supper of *fritto misto,* a mixed fry of little fish from the River Orcia.

Emilio put down his fork in great seriousness. "Maybe some day my big brother will be saint of the animals, like Saint Francis of Assisi," he said proudly. "Then, Babbo, you will not laugh."

Giorgio's eyes glanced up from his plate and found the Palio horse he had made, standing big-chested on a shelf. He saw that the spennacchiera had fallen off, and he got up to press it back in place.

The mother watched him cross the room. "There are many ways," she said softly, "for a boy to bring honor to Monticello."

Her eyes and Giorgio's met and held for a brief instant.

It was late in November when the farm work lessened and the fun began. Hard by the village of Monticello were horse-rearing farms, and often in the afternoons

the older boys who helped in the barns challenged Giorgio to a race. He was quick to accept each time, but he seldom rode the same horse twice. "Never do I want to love one so much," he explained to his father, "the way it was with Bianca, the blind one."

Always he rode bareback, no matter how rough the horse's gaits, and always he used only his left hand on the reins. Some of the horses in the Palio, he had heard, were no better bred than those his father bought and sold. And if they had to be ridden bareback, with the right hand free for the nerbo, he must practice now.

The other boys were older, taller, and they rode by

gripping hard with their legs. But Giorgio had to work for balance, leaning always with his mount, thinking with him, flying together like one streamer in the wind.

The boys soon recognized that Giorgio had a special way with horses. Even the poor ones ran well when he was their fantino, and when he had a good one, he was almost never defeated.

In time the races developed into hard-fought contests held on the winding mountain road. Giorgio's heart sang a high tune as he flew around the curves, his face lashed by his horse's mane. He was in Siena! Riding in the Palio! *This* curve was San Martino, *this* the Casato. The rippling of his horse's muscles against his thighs made him feel like a man-horse, a centaur! He was no longer an earthling; he flew.

With each race the make-believe intensified. The boys pretended they were in the Palio, each riding for his contrada.

"I race for the Eagle!" one would shout.

"I race for the Panther!"

"I for the Wolf!"

"I for the Porcupine!"

It was fun at first, but for Giorgio the make-believe did not last. He saw it for what it was, a pitiful imitation. None of the horses wore spennacchiera in their headstalls. Nor did the fantinos fight with oxhide nerbos. It was no battle at all!

*Chapter VI*

### GIORGIO MEETS A SNAIL

As Giorgio rode to one victory after another, more and more people came to watch. Word of his skill began to travel. It trickled like a wind with a growing strength, first to the little towns on the fringe of the Maremma, then to the foothills of Mount Amiata, and finally it sifted through the mountain passes to the ancient walled city of Siena.

There, at the bottom of a steep, winding street known as Fontebranda, lived a horseman belonging to the Contrada of the Snail. He was owner of some rental properties, farms and homes, and he lived comfortably on the rents they brought in. But what he really lived on was an intangible thing, a pride in his daughter, Anna. For her he would have plucked the moon and the stars. But since she shared his love of horses, he settled for a fine stable. He kept four horses, sometimes five, and he made sure they were burnished like copper, trained by the most skilled, and ridden by men with sensitive hands.

His name was Signor Ramalli. He had never won a Palio, but he never gave up trying. One day in the spring of the year he made an excursion to the Maremma for the express purpose of seeking out a certain horseboy. He did not leave Siena until after his noon meal, and he stopped here and there in villages along the road to buy a bottle of olive oil, a jug of wine, and a brisket of veal; so it was nearing nightfall when he reached the hilltop village of Monticello. He inquired of a cobbler the way to Giorgio's house. The man poked his head into Signor Ramalli's automobile and with a breath rich in garlic directed him up the steep, tortuous lane to a flight of steps flanked by potted geraniums.

When the Signore found the house, there was scarce room enough to park his car nearby, but he managed to wedge it in a crook of space made by several lanes coming together. Then with a smile for the curious children who gathered around, he walked up the worn steps and knocked on the door.

Giorgio's small brother opened it. *"Buona sera,"* he said politely. "I am Emilio. And I have a sister Teria who bosses me, and a big brother who is watchkeeper of the church." All in the same breath he added, "Your vest is nice; it looks like our newborn calf."

"Newborn calf it is!" The man laughed in amusement.

Emilio's mother came hurrying out of the bedroom, tying a fresh apron over her black dress. She saw at a glance that the stranger was a city man from over the mountain.

*"Buona sera,"* she said. "Please to excuse our little Emilio. He chatters like the wren."

Signor Ramalli bowed and removed his hat. "You have an elder son, Giorgio?" he asked.

"Si," the mother replied anxiously. "Has something happened to him?"

"No, no, Signora. Everything is most right."

"Then will you please to come in and have a coffee while you wait? At this moment Giorgio should be in the barn, bedding our donkey. Soon he comes."

"Thank you kindly, but I will go to find him; that is, if you will be so good as to direct me."

The mother stepped out onto the porch. "You go only a little downhill," she said, "just beyond the public fountain. As you go, it is on your right hand. My little Emilio here can take you, but he must hurry back."

Emilio, flushed with importance, took the stranger's hand and led him the short distance to the stable.

"Giorgio!" he called out. "Here is a Signore who wants to see you!" Then reluctantly he turned and headed for home, glancing back at every step.

Giorgio was leading Pippa out between the shafts of the cart. "You come to see me?" he asked of the strange man.

Signor Ramalli stepped up and shook hands briskly. "Go on working, Giorgio, while I talk. From the fragrant smells at your house I believe a good bean soup is simmering, and I must not delay you."

Giorgio pulled the cart to the far end of the stable and tilted the shafts against the wall. The donkey, freed, trotted to an empty manger and in a raucous bray demanded her supper.

Signor Ramalli sized up the boy as he watched him pour out a measure of grain. He could not help thinking how small Giorgio appeared in the bigness of the barn, but he was not going to change his mind now. The boy might be little, yet he was wiry, had good muscle, straight, sturdy legs, and he worked quickly and with purpose. The man laughed softly to himself; he was analyzing the boy as he would a horse!

"I am Ramalli of Siena," he explained. "I am a Snail."

Giorgio spun around. "You are *what?*" He took in the man's features, and saw on his forehead a wen bigger than the bulb on a snail's antenna. Is that why, he wondered, the man calls himself a snail?

"I belong to the Contrada of the Snail."

"Oh?" The word contrada sparked a lightning chain of thought direct to the Palio.

"My main activity is horses and racing."

Giorgio stopped his work. He bowed to the man as if he were a king or a cardinal. Then in his excitement he began scratching the donkey, kneading down the dark stripe along her back. He took a breath, listening.

"I have heard of your skill in racing, and . . ." Signor Ramalli paused to let the full weight of his words take meaning. "I propose that you ride for me."

The boy's heart seemed to stop altogether, then hammered wildly against his chest. Speechless, he waited for more.

"Yes," the man was saying, "I propose that you ride for me in the little races in the provinces."

Giorgio felt suddenly as if he had been dropped into a well. "Wh-wh-where?" he stammered, hoping he had misunderstood.

"In the nearby small towns—in Asciano, in Montalcino, in Poggibonsi, and others. You can continue to work on your father's farm, and come away only on festival days. And you will not need to bother with special racing costume."

Signor Ramalli came forward, and now he too began ruffling Pippa's mane. "Does it not please you?" he asked.

Giorgio blushed, trying to hide his disappointment. In his mind he could hear his father saying, "All in one day Rome was not built! Time it takes to build a city; and time, too, to build a man."

Everything was quiet, except for Pippa's teeth grinding the grain to a mealy mush.

At last Giorgio nodded soberly and replied in a voice he hardly knew as his own. "*Grazie,* Signor Ramalli, I will ride for you."

Across the donkey's back man and boy shook hands.

"In Siena," Signor Ramalli smiled, "each contrada has 'protectors.' Do you know what they are, my boy?" He waited for an answer, but when none came he went on. "A protector is a person who believes in the people of a certain contrada and does all he can to help them; he offers friendship, advice, and money, too. It is a kind of kinship."

"I understand."

"It is my wish now to be protector to the little runt of Monticello!" He smiled again, and the term from his lips took on a note of affection. "In you," he said with a final warm handclasp, "I have great faith."

That night in bed Giorgio lay awake a long time, thrashing out his disappointment. To race in the little festivals was not what he had hoped for; but perhaps— he tried to comfort himself—perhaps it was a beginning.

*Chapter VII*

BRING OUT THE SATCHEL!

Giorgio's disappointment vanished with his first race. In the company of a strong, willing horse how could he be anything but sublimely happy? Compared to the lesser creatures he raced against, the entries he rode for Signor Ramalli were always in top condition, sleek and fit. And so, nearly always he won.

The entire family basked in Giorgio's good fortune. He brought home trinkets and treats from hilltown and valley. From Asciano one evening he burst into the kitchen with an armful of surprises for everyone—a singing canary for Teria, three goldfish for Emilio, a brooch for his mother, and a pouch of tobacco for his father; even a mouse toy for Mom-cat and her kittens. For himself he had bought a shiny new flute with extra stops.

Later that evening, with the younger children in bed and the supper dishes done, the mother turned to Giorgio. "Now then," she spoke in delighted anticipation, "stop playing your flute, close the light, and come tell to Babbo and me how you won at Asciano. In the dark," she added, "our mind goes to the place and we live better those moments with you. Besides, it saves the electricity."

White moonlight flooded the room. It silhouetted the father, comfortable on the couch, head leaning against the wall, pipe jutting out in sharp profile. Now and then it belched a little shower of sparks.

"I did not win today," Giorgio announced.

If he had flung a stick of dynamite into the room, the effect could not have been greater.

"No! Oh no!" the mother cried in dismay. "Where then came the money for birds and brooches and fish? Where? Where!"

The father jerked bolt upright. His mouth fell open, and the pipe clattered to the floor. "How can this be?" he demanded. "Explain yourself, boy!"

Giorgio deliberately lifted his flute and tootled a string of giddy notes to the faraway mountains. Then he laid it down. "*I* did not win," he said simply. "My horse won. I was passenger only."

"Bravo! Bravo!" The father laughed in relief. "Of you I am proud. Man should not pump himself up when the victory is not his own."

From his first days of racing, Giorgio felt himself a man. He changed from short pants to long. He had his hair cut oftener and kept it slicked back to discourage the waviness. He walked more erect, trying to make himself taller.

All summer long he was excused from farmwork whenever a race was held nearby. Signor Ramalli himself seldom attended, but when he did, he was accompanied by little Anna. The two of them shouted and cheered so lustily that it seemed to Giorgio his horse sailed in on the sound waves of their voices.

Summer spent itself. The time of harvest came again to the Maremma. And afterward the wind blew cold and the autumn rains sluiced down the mountains, making rivers of the little streams. Giorgio and his father no longer went to the farm, and for now, racing days were over and done with.

To help out the family, Giorgio went to work for the town cobbler. It was interesting at first to learn to use a lapstone and awl, and it was fun to sew with a pig's whisker, driving it like a dagger in and out of the leather. As he worked, he made believe that the tap-tap of the cobbler's hammer was the tattoo of horses' hoofs.

In a few days, however, the newness wore off. Then the tiny shop became a prison. It closed in on him, choking off his breath. The tap-tap never varied from trot to gallop to walk. It was deadly monotonous, always the same—tap-tap-tap-tap—until some days his head was fit to burst. As the door and then the single window had to be closed against the increasing cold, the pungent smells of turpentine and benzine and neatsfoot oil were almost more than he could bear. All these, mixed with the perspiration of feet and the garlic of the cobbler's breath, made a stench that lingered in Giorgio's nostrils long after he reached home.

As if this were not torment enough, he often made mistakes at his bench—riling a heel unevenly so the wearer walked quite unbalanced and raised a storm of protest; or hammering nails so they protruded inside the sole and gave no end of discomfort. For these blunders, he sometimes had to forfeit most of his meager pay.

But at last the winter days dragged to a close, and all at once spring came in with a rush and a flood. Melting snows bubbled and boiled down the mountainsides. Fruit trees exploded in white popcorn buds. Birds gathered up more straws than their beaks could hold.

Giorgio felt like a bird, too, a bird suddenly released from its cage. Once again he and his father were out in the fields. Each worked with a zest to his own goal, the father to win the land, the boy to harden his muscles, to increase his wind power. They ate with the same spirit and gusto, opening the lunch bag as if it held the secret to more power and strength.

"We stoke and stoke to make the hotter fire! Not so, Giorgio?" Babbo asked every noon. And they laughed as their hands broke open the crisp loaf of bread and their hard white teeth bit into it and then into a chunk of wild boar sausage. Noisily they chewed them both together so that the deliciousness of one brought out the deliciousness of the other. Some days there was a good thick pea soup as a surprise. Then they sang a rollicking blessing after instead of before their meal.

"We bellow out so deep from the soul," the father chuckled, "that God in His heaven can hear without even pushing aside the clouds. Eh, son?" And they both roared in laughter.

Afterward they lay down on the earth and snored like tired animals.

Plowing. Harrowing. Seeding. No task too big, none too small. And always in the twilight hours Giorgio's feet unerringly took him around to the horse barn. Some inner need urged him, drove him, compelled him to gallop into the sunset as regularly as he ate or slept. Was it a need to flaunt his freedom from earth and cobbler's shop? Or to give the horses a taste of Paradise before they went to the butcher's block? He did not know. He knew only that at day's end when he was sweaty, dirt-creased, and limp, he found joy in thundering across the swales as if in the next moment he and his horse could float over the mountain and into the sky.

The seasons wore on. The festivals came again, and again Giorgio rode for Signor Ramalli. The Umbrella Man came and went, and with his coming the Palio dream intensified, yet remained always the same— always beautiful, always on the other side of the mountain, always out of reach. Winter closed in and the days in the cobbler's shop piled up endlessly, one on top of another, and all were alike.

One day in the following spring, Giorgio felt as if his life had come to a standstill. He seemed to be marking time, doing the same things over and over and over again, working each summer in the fields, riding each fall in little unimportant races, sweating out each winter in the cobbler's shop. He was like a turnspit dog, running in a treadmill cage, smelling the roast but never tasting it.

In this mood of despair he arrived home to find the family in a high state of excitement. They met him at the door, all speaking at once.

"A letter! A letter! A letter!"

"For you comes a letter!"

"It says: 'Sig. Terni Giorgio.'"

"Open it, quick!"

Everyone waited on Giorgio as if he were king. Emilio hung up his lunch bag after fingering inside for the crumbs. Teria brought him a cup of hot coffee.

The mother handed him one of her long hairpins. "Here, Giorgio, with this you have a fine letter opener."

The father entered unnoticed. "Is it no more the habit in this house to greet the father come home from work?"

Hurriedly the children showered him with hugs, then ran back to Giorgio.

"Let *me* open it!" shouted Emilio.

"No," Signora Terni said firmly. "It is Giorgio's."

Giorgio stood very still. He took the letter and the hairpin with trembling hands. The blood throbbed in his head. He had once received flute music sent from Rome, but that was in a thin roll with his name printed by machine. This was a real letter, handwritten in black ink.

"Don't stab too deep," the mother warned. "You might cut also the paper inside."

Cautiously, as if a Jack-in-the-box might pop out, Giorgio slit the envelope. He unfolded the fine white paper and silently read the few lines. His face paled, then flushed.

"What is it?" asked the mother in alarm.

"What does it say?" cried Teria.

"The news, is it good?" asked Babbo.

"Is it bad?" shouted Emilio.

If Mount Amiata had suddenly risen from its base and marched across the valley, Giorgio could not have been more amazed. "It's from Signor Ramalli! Never before has he written me!"

"Read it out," cried Teria.

Giorgio cleared his throat and read slowly:

"Siena, 16 March, 1952

"Dear Giorgio:

"If your Babbo can spare you from the fields, I desire you to come at once to Siena. I have now four extraordinary horses and would wish you to be their trainer. The Palio of July, as you know, is on the second. We must hurry.

"Expecting you soon, I am,

V. Ramalli"

Grown as he was, Giorgio grasped Emilio by one fat hand and swung him around and around until the pots and pans on the wall went flying. Then he swooped up the letter and held it on high as if it were the Palio banner itself.

"Mammina!" he cried. "Everybody! Everybody! Bring out the satchel. I go to Siena."

## Chapter VIII

### OVER THE MOUNTAIN

Babbo rose to his feet. In the darkening room his eyes gleamed in pride. "I have gooseflesh! I cannot believe it could be! Today a letter is come. Tomorrow our Giorgio goes over the mountain. To please Signor Ramalli," he declared, "he must arrive in Siena tomorrow."

Plans were quickly made. It was decided that in his new importance Giorgio should not walk the long way to Casalino to catch the autobus that would carry him to the train at Sant' Angelo, and thence to Siena. Instead, the entire family would drive him in the donkey cart directly to Sant' Angelo, where they could all bid him good-bye at the railway station.

It happened just so. Even Pippa took part, giving out a steamwhistle bray that nearly drowned the conductor's cry of "Ready!"

As the train pulled away, Giorgio leaned far out the window, waving his satchel. Wistfully, he watched Mamma and Babbo, Teria and Emilio climb into the donkey cart, and his eyes held them there together until nothing was left, nothing but a tiny blur against the yellow of the station. Then that, too, was gone.

Hands still clutching his satchel, he kept right on standing in the aisle, staring out at the fast-moving landscape. And all at once the hollow pain in his stomach left him, and he faced the bigness of his adventure. It was as though the rushing wind and the chugging engine were taking possession of him, lifting him out of himself, over the mountain, and into a new world.

The cone of Mount Amiata loomed ahead with clouds toppling along its ridges, and streams spilling whitely down its face and into the river below. Still at the open window, he could feel the train laboring on its long climb from the valley of the Orcia to the folded hills. He saw with surprise that it was not just one valley, but a succession of countless hills and vales. Like an earthworm the train wriggled through them, and up through a wilderness of boulders broken only by tufts of broom and brush.

He saw the kilns of charcoal burners, and a goat girl

knitting as she watched her flock, and he saw stunted sheep scrabbling upward toward the mountain pastures. He was glad he was not a sheep, nibbling his slow way to the top. And he was gladder still when the desert of rock gave way to dark forests of chestnut trees, and then to beech, and then to scrub pine. The little hills were ridges now, and as fast as the train could make the turns it pushed on up steeper and steeper ascents until it reached the summit, the bleak bare summit where the sharp wind held a bitterness that made his eyes weep.

"Boy!" The voice of an old woman startled him. "Close that window, if you please. My old bones shudder with the cold. Besides, your face grows red and smudged."

Giorgio quickly closed the window, wiped his face on his new handkerchief, and found a seat. He placed his satchel between his legs and tirelessly scanned the horizon as the train began to roll down out of the high country. Every frowning castle in the distance, every bold fortress, every hamlet he mistook for the city of his dream. But when at last he caught his first glimpse, he knew it for Siena, yet was unprepared for its splendor. In the clearness of early evening the jewel-like city rose up on the shoulders of three hills, its slender towers jutting into the sky. They were like none he had ever seen. One was shining white with stripings of black, like a zebra; the others were pink and carmine, or was this rosy color a trick of the setting sun?

His heart raced. He felt her ancientness at once. Here were battlemented walls, and pinnacled domes, and steeples piled high and higher—all jumbled, yet ordered.

Siena! Siena!

It was the hour of early evening when the train pulled into the station. Giorgio was first to jump out. He hurried through the groups of waiting people, impatient to find Signor Ramalli. Searching faces, hoping to see one he dared ask directions, he threaded the network of narrow streets. The people seemed different to him, like figures in a painting. He wondered if they might even speak a different language!

Slight-built as he was, he kept clumsily bumping into the passers-by. Each time he tried to work up his courage to ask, but no one took notice of him. It was like walking in sleep until a deep-timbered voice broke into it.

"Young lad! Come here!" The voice belonged to the Chief-of-the-Town-Guards. He was an enormous man, handsome in a dark blue uniform with gold epaulets. "Young lad, you will find better the walking if you move with, not against, the promenaders. Now," he asked solicitously, "can I help you?"

Giorgio felt a surge of relief. They spoke the same language! "Signor Ramalli," he burst out, "his house I must find. If you please!"

The Chief-of-the-Guards looked down from his

great height. "To find Signor Ramalli's house," he said, "you have only to follow your nose."

"My nose?"

"Yes," he laughed, "your nose. You go down and down the Via Fontebranda, and when your nose is stinging with the stench of animal hides in brine, then you are there. Almost." He held on to Giorgio with one white-gloved hand while with the other he stopped an autobus to let by a team of scrawny horses drawing a load of wood.

"Feed the bony beasts," he cried to the portly driver, "instead of yourself!"

Then he turned again to Giorgio. "Now, young man, after the smell from the slaughterhouse you will run into a new smell of lye and bleach from the public laundry. Then turn in at the next doorway, and there you are!"

Giorgio hesitated. "But *my* Signor Ramalli must have a stable."

"Yes, yes, I know," the Chief replied in friendly annoyance. "It is as I said. Through the bad smells you must go until you come to the nice fragrance of horses and hay. You see, lad, the house of the Ramallis is at the end of the street, with magnificent vista of the valley beyond."

No directions were ever given more clearly. Down, down the Via Fontebranda Giorgio hurried half-running, not to get past the cow hides in brine, but because the descent was almost perpendicular.

Just as the Chief had said, the last door belonged to the Ramallis. The family of three welcomed him as if he were a son come home. They were in the dining room, and at once the mother and daughter arose to set an extra place.

Signor Ramalli hooked his thumbs into his calf vest and smiled at Giorgio. "After we eat, we give you choice of two rooms for your sleeping quarters. One is in our home, and the other is the empty storeroom over the stable where you can hear the slightest whinny in the night. That room, though barer, is bigger and . . ."

"I would rather prefer the storeroom," Giorgio interrupted, "where I can be closer to my horses."

It was, in fact, a tremendous room. It faced the east where the first rays of the sun came slanting in, touching off the strings of purple onions and garlic, and peppers, shiny red. Besides these gay decorations there was a wide and comfortable brass bed, a trestle table and chair, and an ancient sea chest that had been emptied for Giorgio's clothes.

Comfortable as his room was, it was only a place to sleep. Sixteen hours of the day he lived with his horses. There were three mares and a gelding depending on him for all the creature comforts of food and water, and new shoes, and warm blankets at night, and small friendly talk.

But more, Signor Ramalli was depending on him to bring them all into bloom for the July Palio. This was high challenge. Here he was, still a boy in his teens, barely shoulder-high to his pupils; yet he was master of their destiny! Ambra needed schooling in being mounted; a race could be lost before it began. Lubiana was stubborn, always wanting her own way. Dorina was awkward at maneuvering; she could lose the Palio at the hairpin turns.

Imperiale, however, posed the most interesting problem. He was a big-going fellow, part Arabian, sired by the famous Sans Souci. What he needed was soothing words to quiet his nervous habit of biting on the wood of his stall. He reminded Giorgio of a frightened child chewing his fingernails.

Each day Signor Ramalli grew more pleased with Giorgio. The boy was two persons in one—skilled trainer in the morning; stableboy in the afternoon. He attacked the cleaning of the stalls, the oiling of the bridle leathers, the currying and grooming with the same chin-thrust of determination as he did the fine art of teaching.

And so, nothing was good enough for him. Morning and night, he ate at table with the family, but this, instead of making him feel jolly, stirred up the beginnings of homesickness. There was something about Anna that reminded him not of his sister, Teria, but of Emilio—a kind of puckish eagerness, wanting to know about the horses, wanting to help, wanting to ride.

It was after supper, after darkness, that doubt and anguish and the sharp pangs of homesickness set in in earnest. His dream of the Palio seemed as far away as ever. "I am only an outsider," he thought as he sat alone and forlorn on the sea chest. "I belong to no contrada, for I am not born Sienese. There are seventeen contradas, yet no one of them has asked me to ride. I have four horses, but I have none." He smiled a crooked smile, recalling how he had longed to be in Siena, but now that he was here something had gone wrong with the dream.

In humiliation and despair, his homesickness washed over him like a wave, and he could see the Maremma where earth and sea and sky come together, and the earth's humps that form Mount Amiata. And in all that wild sweep the only man-made thing was the cross on the mountain. In his loneness he closed his eyes, and there were the warm, smoke-wreathed rooms at home, and in the smoke he saw the whole family, clustered about a sausage hanging from the kitchen ceiling. Each in turn was rubbing a slice of bread against it for flavor because the meat itself had to be saved for supper. Yet in the poverty there was a closeness and understanding he now missed. For moments he seemed unable to breathe; it was the same tight, suffocating feeling he had known in the cobbler's shop.

The only help was to run, run, run! Night after night this need took possession of him. Like a colt spooked by an imaginary devil he bolted out of his room, raced up through the canyon walls of Fontebranda, across the busy Via di Città, down a flight of steps, and out onto the vast and beautiful Piazza del Campo. Here he could look up above the circle of turreted palaces and see a wide patch of sky and the same old dipper that winked down on Monticello, and all at once he felt less alone. Gulping and panting, he could squeeze the heaviness out of his lungs, could breathe in cool fresh air.

Night after night he had to escape, always to the deep stillness of the Piazza. It became his habit to stand first before the dazzling Fonte Gaia, admiring the frieze of white marble statues in their white marble niches, and the marble wolves spewing water into the marble pool. Then he would face about and look across the broad shell of the amphitheater to the Palazzo Pubblico, where the city officials worked, and his eyes went up and up its soaring tower until he imagined he saw a bell ringer away up there, no bigger than a spider.

He tried not to torture himself by studying the race course around the empty shell, or wondering which contrada might some day choose him as their fantino. Instead, his mind went back to the years before the Palio, when men battled bulls in the square. If he half-closed his eyes, he could array himself in coat of mail and he could see the blade of his spear flashing silver in the moonlight as he thrust it into the flesh of a charging bull. Then heavy with weariness, as if he had slain a score of bulls, he trudged back to his room and slept.

But in sleep he could not wear the blinders. His dreams were always of the Palio.

As the first month wore itself out, Signor Ramalli

sensed a growing restlessness in the boy. One day he recognized it openly.

"Tomorrow," he said to Giorgio, "is a Sunday. A quick journey to Monticello is the best cure I know for ailments like homesickness. In a day you will come back feeling more content here. Now then, in the morning when I get out my car to take my wife and Anna to the early mass, I will at the same time take you to the station. My wife will prepare for you a little lunch to carry, and I will buy you a ticket, both ways."

He held out his hand. Giorgio put his small calloused one inside the great warmth of the Signore's and felt it close around his with a clasp so strong it made him blink. Giorgio's heart leaped in joy.

*Chapter IX*

## THE CART HORSE OF CASALINO

The Sunday train inched its way along toward the Maremma. Instead of *Accelerato* it should be called the tortoise, Giorgio thought. He paced up and down the aisle. He leaned out the window, waving at peasants working in the fields even on a Sunday. He ate his lunch—thick slices of ham with white bread, and an orange. He took off his jacket and shadowboxed with a fat little boy.

At Sant' Angelo he changed to an autobus and finally, toward noon, arrived at the crossroads of Casalino.

It was one of those freakish days in late spring when

the air seems to belong to July. The sun brassy hot, the wind at a standstill. No one was anywhere in sight except a carter, a big loutish fellow with an ear trumpet hanging on a string around his neck.

"Hey, boy," the man called out. "For two hundred lire I carry you . . . wherever."

Giorgio felt for the two hundred lire in his pocket. Did the man sitting in that rickety old cart have X-ray eyes to make up for his bad ears?

"No, no, thank you," Giorgio replied. "Only a few kilometers I must walk." He started to explain where he was going, and perhaps if the driver seemed friendly he might even confide that the two hundred lire had been saved for a special sugar bowl in a special cupboard in a special house in Monticello. But he stopped short as his eye fell upon the mare hitched to the cart. She had something of the look of his Imperiale, only finer-boned and more Arab. She was a gray, flecked with brown, but too thin by far and her coat dry and harsh.

He wondered if it was the way she jibbed her head and nervously pawed the earth, or just the general look of her that put him in mind of Imperiale. Or was it the wide-set eyes, so dark and smoldering?

"Excuse," he said, stepping up close to the man and mouthing his words slowly, "but the mare—is she by Sans Souci?"

"Eh?" The driver adjusted his ear trumpet, cocking his head in puzzlement. "Eh?"

"I say, is she by Sans Souci?"

"Si, si. She for sale."

"I don't want to buy her. I only ask . . ."

"Nobody want to buy her. She spring like cat, kick like kangaroo, chip wood like woodpecker." He started to goad her with the whip; then, as her ears laced back, he changed his mind. He turned to the boy abruptly. "Who are you?" he asked.

"I am Giorgio Terni."

The slit mouth widened in a grin. "O-o-oh, you're Tullio Terni's boy, the little runt of Monticello. For you I cut my price; for one hundred lire I carry you to door of house."

Giorgio smiled his thanks and turned away. He set off down the road, twice looking over his shoulder at the fine Arab head with the small ears pricked against the sky. He thought he heard a nervous whinny, but it might have been the breeze in the poplars.

He strode to Monticello as if there were springs inside him. Along the way people welcomed him, called him by name. "Hi, Giorgio, how is it being a city fellow?"

But the real welcome came within the encompassing walls of home. To his family he was already a hero. They fluttered about him, taking off his jacket, pouring him coffee, peppering him with questions.

"How do they treat you? Do you get nice white bread with your meals, and is the spaghetti cooked done? Do you get used to those noisy streets?" This was Mamma talking.

"Do you like Anna more than me?" This was Teria.

"Did you bring me something? A calf vest, maybe? Is the bump still on Signor Ramalli's forehead?" This was Emilio.

And at long last, from Babbo, the question Giorgio wanted first: "How do you get along with the training of the horses? Tell us all about."

"We-ll-ll," Giorgio answered importantly, "I have four horses in my stable. I get along pretty well. Of course, there are some difficulties. First I have Ambra. She is fine, but has strong dislike for bridling. Then I have Lubiana, who is fine too, but sometimes stubborn like mule. And Dorina, she is awkward in changing gaits."

He saved the best until last. "And I have Imperiale. He is Arab, and he flies!" He turned his chair to face his father. "Now it is I who ask. Babbo! I saw today at Casalino a mare, gray and lightly specked with brown. She is poor and thin, and she pulls a miserable cart with traces and harness held together by rope. But she looks to be one of San Souci's get."

"She is!" exclaimed the father.

Giorgio's heart was a hammer. He could hardly wait to tell Signor Ramalli that now he was a real horseman. His questions came fast.

"How old is she?

"From where does she come?

"Why is she not racing instead of pulling the cart?

"Has she colts?"

The father scraped his chair away from the table. He reached for the stool in front of the cupboard and propped his stockinged feet on it. He loosened his belt and gave a happy grunt. It was good to have man talk in the house again!

"That poor mare," he began, folding his hands across his stomach, "is sold for convenience from one to the other. She has the nervous tic, so that forever she is biting—on wood, on anything. And her throat . . ."

"I know, Babbo. It makes the throat swell." The father nodded, proud of his son's knowledge. "Men beat her, thinking it will stop the biting, but it only gets worse. Now she is good just for carting things from here to there."

Teria interrupted to place before Giorgio a slice of ham and an onion, and the mother brought out a whole loaf of white bread, newly baked and still warm.

"Do you want the crust, Giorgio, or just a thin slice?"

"The crust as always, Mamma, if you please."

"Emilio!" commanded the father. "Your brother cannot eat without a good glass of wine."

Fearful of missing a word, Emilio flew to the grotto of a cellar behind the front steps and returned breathless with a dusty old flask.

Giorgio was busy scooping out a little hollow in the crust with the point of his knife.

"What you doing, Giorgio?" asked the father. "You not eating the ham?"

"No, thank you," he said, noticing how little was left. "I am just hungry to taste again our onions cut up in the crust with vinegar and salt, and maybe some capers, if we have . . ."

The capers appeared as if by magic from Teria's hand.

Between bites, Giorgio interrupted the silence which surrounded him. "But why," he asked of Babbo, "do they sell that mare from one to the other? Is it the nervous tic?"

The father pursed his lips, thinking.

"That can be controlled," Giorgio added quickly. "The great Sans Souci had it, and my Imperiale has it, too. Is it only because of that?"

"No." The father paused.

"What, then?"

"Well, you can't believe it, but ill luck trails her like smoke from fire. Already she has four colts of no account."

"Four!"

The father nodded. "The first time she got twins, but they died before lifting their heads above the straw."

"And then?"

"Next time her colt is crippled in foaling and has to be put down."

Giorgio stopped eating and sat silent. After a moment he said, "And the fourth colt? Dead, too?"

"No. Not him. He will make big stout plow horse when he is grown. He is no more like Farfalla than bull is like deer."

The mother, who had been listening all this while, now plucked at Giorgio's sleeve. "Farfalla is the one . . ." she whispered softly. "She is the one born in Magliano Toscano on the day Bianca . . ."

Giorgio felt the hairs on his skin prickle. So this Arab mare, fastened with ropes to the traces of a shabby cart, was Bianca's successor! He nodded and smiled wistfully in remembrance.

The next morning Giorgio was back at work in Siena, happier and more content there. And for the first time he felt encouraged that Dorina and Imperiale might be ready for the July Palio. As he schooled the well-bred gelding, teaching him to make smaller and ever smaller turns, his mind flew back to the cart horse of Casalino. Clear as a vignette he saw her jibbing her head against the sky.

"It would be a miracle from God," he thought to himself, "to harness that wildness, to calm the frightened soul."

## Chapter X

### A BUYER OF OX SKINS

It was on the day Giorgio returned to Siena that Farfalla was sold again. A buyer of ox skins, Signor Busisi by name, was making one of his regular trips to the Maremma. He was a big-framed, bushy-browed man with a shock of white hair. As he drove along in his shiny new Fiat, he was sorting skins in his mind— all sizes, all qualities. He was not even thinking about horses. And he was trying very hard not to notice his nagging indigestion.

Signor Busisi was from Siena, and therefore he was

first of all a strong contrada man with a passion for the Palio. Besides, he was a canny judge of horseflesh. In years past his horses had won no less than five Palio banners, a record few owners could match! And when he had no entry for the Palio, he sat as a judge of the trials, helping to choose the ten horses that would run, out of the twenty or more presented. His fellow judges held him in great respect, often waiting for him to nod the decisive "yes" or "no."

Of course, being an honest man and a realistic one, Signor Busisi admitted to himself that over the years he had purchased some weedy horses with faults too numerous and embarrassing to think about. And so he did not think about them. Besides, he was getting on in years, trying to ignore the pains around his heart and the frequent attacks of indigestion. "I've got a lot of age on me," he told himself. "No time for regrets; for me the spring flowers will bloom only a few times more. Better it is to look *ahead*." And so in the years remaining he was determined to live each day as if it were the last to shine upon him.

On this morning of April the Maremma country was the color of clear emeralds, the birds singing, and nothing between earth and sky except, coming over the hill ahead, a tall, airy-striding cart horse.

The Signore slowed down and pulled off to the edge of the road. He got out and unbuckled his belt a notch. The pangs of indigestion were sharpening. Perhaps walking around a bit, exchanging the time of day with a country carter, might ease the pain.

Before he greeted the man, he unconsciously took stock of the mare. To himself he said, "She must be well over sixteen hands high. Good legs and feet. Fine bone beneath the rough coat. Barrel too thin, head and throttle excellent. Eyes dominant."

The carter meanwhile was sizing up the automobile and the owner. "Is new—the car. Is old—the man. And rich. I wonder, will he permit that I haul goods for him from here to there?"

"*Buon giorno,*" Signor Busisi said in a loud voice, noticing the ear trumpet.

The carter bowed until his chin touched his grease-stained shirt.

"Your mare," the Signore began, "how is she called?"

"Si, si. She for sale."

"Not so quick, my good man," the Signore bellowed. "I only ask how you call her."

The carter was unabashed. He grinned, showing yellow, horselike teeth. "She has the name Farfalla. She is daughter from Maremma mare and Sans Souci."

"Incredible!" the Signore exclaimed. "That accounts for the quality look."

"Eh?" the driver asked, holding up his trumpet.

"Incredible!"

The grin widened. "How long you stay in Maremma?"

"Today only."

The carter scratched his nose thoughtfully. Money jingling in his pocket and wine on the table would be better than a no-good mare. "Signore," he said in a nasal, wheedling voice, "you like buy my mare?"

Signor Busisi made no answer. At close range he saw that she was no longer young. "What age has she?" he asked.

"Eh?"

"How many years has she?"

"Oh, she very young. She has only four years," the man boasted, smiling at his deception.

Signor Busisi ignored the answer. There was that certain something about her—perhaps it was the arch of the neck and the high-flowing tail, perhaps it was the enormousness of the eyes. But somehow, in spite of her rough coat and her shoes too big and the ramshackle cart, in spite of everything, she had dignity and nobility.

The Signore felt that the carter and he, himself, suffered by comparison.

All at once his indigestion was gone! Excitement caught hold of him. He did not want another horse for his own; he felt himself too old. But he was not too old to place her, to give her a chance. She could be good, even great. "Who knows without the trial?" he asked himself.

Sensing a quick sale, the carter was like a tiger cat sniffing its prey. And agile as the cat he leaped from the cart—eyes greedy, hands ready. He held out the reins.

"Not yet! Not yet!" Signor Busisi protested. "I make only the offer."

"And I only look at her shoes," the carter lied. "A stone maybe is caught. I take best care of Farfalla. Always I stop to clean out her feet."

"I am certain you do."

"What you say you give me?"

"I did not say. But I do now. I will give sixty thousand lire."

The carter sneered. "Six thousand lire!" he shouted angrily. "More money I could get for one old, deaf, mangy donkey with red blotches and no hair." He spat on the ground with as much venom as if he had hit the man with his spittle.

Signor Busisi remained unruffled, waiting for a noisy motorcycle to go by. "I said *sixty* thousand lire," he repeated, more loudly this time.

The change in the carter was electric. He bowed low, kissing the Signore's hand.

Quick as a flash the mare took advantage of her owner's bent position. She drew back her lips, and with her big teeth pinched hard through the seat of his trousers.

"Ee-ee-ee-ow!" he screeched, trying in vain to break the viselike grip. It was only by the intervention of the laughing Signor Busisi that she let go.

Rubbing his bruised flesh, the carter promptly agreed that for the sum of sixty thousand lire he would deliver the mare to Siena in a day or two.

Signor Busisi suddenly felt young and strong again. Trying to suppress his laughter, he jackknifed his big frame into his car, swung into the road and roared on to Casalino, thinking, planning, dreaming. Somehow he would do it again—bring the right man and the right horse together. It was a never-failing source of wonderment to him how it came about. That black gelding he had sold to a man of the clergy, and the trick sorrel to a clown in the circus . . .

His thoughts broke off. He was nearing the warehouse where the ox skins would be already dried and dressed, awaiting his selection. He must put the mare out of his mind; and he did. For the time being.

*Chapter XI*

THE GHOST IN THE WAREHOUSE

Eager to make the sale, the carter of Casalino delivered the mare to Siena within the week. And while he went to a restaurant and ordered himself a heaping plate of veal scallopini in anticipation of the sixty thousand lire, Signor Busisi went to the bank to draw out the money.

On his way up the few stairs to the grilled portal, the Signore found himself side by side with a slight young man. He turned to see who it might be, and his face lighted. "Doctor Celli!" he exclaimed in pleased recognition. He hooked his arm through the young man's, swung him around, and led him back down the steps to the courtyard.

"Doctor Celli!" he beamed, unable to conceal his delight. "Think of my bumping into Fate twice in one week! May I delay you a moment? No?"

The gray eyes in the sun-browned face smiled. "Naturally, Signor Busisi. For you, my work can always wait."

"I had not thought to find you so soon."

"To find me?"

"Yes, you. This life is a big puzzle, Celli, jumbled with odd-shaped pieces. Then *presto*, the pieces, they fit!"

"Am I one of the odd pieces?" the doctor laughed.

"Let us say you were."

"And the other?"

"The other piece is . . ." the Signore ran his fingers through his shaggy white hair. Then he straightened to his full height and spoke in staccato excitement. "The other piece is an Arabian mare. She is called by the name Farfalla, and she moves as easily as an oiled machine. I found her in the Maremma. Quite by happenstance." The words now came more slowly. "Doctor Celli, you are the one to prescribe for her. She has the nervous tic."

The young man burst into fresh laughter. "Do you forget, Signore, I am a doctor of accounting, not of medicine?"

"I know, I know; but a doctor of this or that is smart enough to work magic in other fields. Besides, you are a horseman. You have a villa and hunting reserves, and as I recall, there is on your farm a good road, long and straight, fit for gallops. And," he paused a moment in his eagerness, "in less than three months, the Palio!"

The two men in the courtyard stood facing a statue, very tall, of Bandini, a celebrated economist, but neither one saw it. Nor were they conscious of the people going in and out of the bank. They were both seeing the same vision: Piazza del Campo in battle array—flags flying, lances gleaming, knights and nobles marching, horses dancing at the ropes, fantinos tense and ready. In their veins all of the ancient feelings boiled up again.

For a long moment the silence seemed unbreakable. Then at last Signor Busisi exploded. "You, Celli! You belong to the Contrada of the Unicorn. No?"

"Si, si."

"Your contrada is small and has won few Palios. No?"

Again the young man agreed.

"How sad for you, but . . ." the Signore waved his arms to heaven, "think how sweet your frenzy if a horse owned by you should win, even for another contrada!"

"A thousand times I thank you, Signor Busisi, but I never buy the cat in the bag."

"But, Celli! You do not have to buy the cat in the bag. This Farfalla by Sans Souci is here, right here in Siena! You have only to look!"

• • •

Respecting Signor Busisi as he did, Doctor Celli went early the next morning to see Farfalla. She was stabled temporarily in an old, dank warehouse used for storing ox hides. As he left the sunlight and crossed the doorsill, he stood blinking among the flies and the smells of dried blood and brine. A chill went through him. Out of the shadowy darkness the figure of the mare loomed like a gray ghost. Suddenly she scented the stranger and reared into the air, as if she would pitch him heels over head if he tried to mount. Then she retreated into a corner, her ears laid flat, her nostrils snorting, her lips drawn back.

It was several moments before Doctor Celli's eyes became accustomed to the dark. Then he took note of

the fresh teeth marks on the wooden crib. "This crib-
bing is a thing she will not outgrow," he warned himself.
"Yet nervous horses are like nervous people; they work in
bursts of energy. For a race, this is good."

Back and forth he argued with himself. "She is too old
to buy! Already she looks to be a six- or seven-year-old!"

And he answered himself. "But some horses come
late to their full glory." He remembered the mighty
Lipizzans of Vienna whose training did not begin until
they were six. Perhaps she, too, would be a late bloomer.
And if she was daughter to the noble Sans Souci, and if
Signor Busisi liked her, that was enough.

He heard a cough behind him, and turned to find
the Signore standing silently in the doorway.

"Restive, she is," the Signore said, "and pitifully
underfed. But the Arabian blood is unmistakable; no?"

Already Doctor Celli had taken the hurdles in his
mind. "Signor Busisi," he said, "from the fresh teeth
marks it is plain that she is a nervous cribber. You
already have told me this. Yet in spite of it, her possibilities intrigue me."

"Ah," the Signore replied, a wistful note in his voice,
"is it not something beautiful to offer her the chance of
fulfillment in this life?"

Within the span of the next ten minutes the walls of
the warehouse echoed with excited voices. The haggling
over the price began in a series of crescendos—up down,
up down, up down.

The louder the talk, the quieter Farfalla became. The hubbub seemed to be the very balm she needed, and Signor Busisi was quick to point it out. "Notice, Celli," he laughed, "the mare is now tranquil."

At last the two men were shaking hands to seal their agreement, both looking tremendously pleased.

The Signore took a deep breath, feeling his tired old heart skip a beat. "The pieces of the puzzle, they fit nice and precise," he sighed. "For sheer happiness my heart is bursting." And he smiled, as if he had given to the mare and the man their destiny.

As smoke lifts in an uprising wind, so ill fortune lifted for Farfalla. She began a new life. From the dingy, malodorous warehouse she was suddenly living on a windbrushed hilltop beyond the city walls. It was from gloom to Paradise!

She had a nice box stall with sparrows for company, and outside her door she could hear pigs rooting and geese making friendly clacking noises. From her stable a grass-grown lane wound down and leveled off, straight as a string. The stretch of straightness began at a small bridge and flowed quietly through woods and farmland.

Each day was like the one before, and they were all good. Mornings when the mist lay wet and shining upon the land, she was saddled and bridled, and away she trotted without the nuisance of a cart joggling along behind. No rumbly noises at all. And no collar across her shoulders, nor leathers holding her back. Only a light hand on the reins and the light weight of Doctor Celli in the saddle. Occasionally a span of oxen would loom into sight and plod by, but to Farfalla they were placid old friends, remembered from the Maremma.

In this pleasant way the days and weeks of training for the Palio slipped by, one like the other. But along toward the end of June, with the selection of the horses only three days away, Doctor Celli was sent on a business errand to Rome. Scarcely had he left Siena when the sky clouded and the rain began. It pelted down in big drops, far apart at first, then closer and closer until they formed a thick curtain. Hour on hour the rain drummed ceaselessly against the small window of Farfalla's stable, until the noise and the eerie darkness threw her into a terror. She jerked her head up and down, more desperate with each moment, and she clamped her teeth on the uprights of her stall, biting them, peeling slivers of wood, and at the same time sucking in great mouthfuls of air.

Night and morning, the tenant farmer sloshed through the rain to look in on her. He saw to it that she had fresh water and grain and sweet meadow hay. But he cut his visits short, for she reared and snorted at the shadows made by his lantern, and her ghost-white color made his own flesh creep. He noticed her appetite was poor, but he attributed it to the foul weather and the lack of exercise. What he failed to notice was the swelling of her throat, and her belly becoming hard and distended.

When Doctor Celli returned, on the evening of the second day, he hurried at once to the stable. It was the very eve before the selection of the horses, and he wanted to be sure that Farfalla was as fit and happy as he had left her. With his hat dripping and his raincoat glossy wet, he entered her stall. To his horror he found her rolling from side to side, pawing the air in an agony of pain. He called in a veterinarian at once, but with all the aids of stomach pump and quieting medicines she still could not be readied in time for the trials.

*Chapter XII*

REJECTED

On his way to the trials the next morning Giorgio Terni heard the news, but it carried no weight with him. He was riding Dorina to the Piazza del Campo to present her before the august body of judges. As he drew rein at a busy corner, he saw the tall figure of the Chief-of-the-Guards and heard his deep voice ring out:

"*Attenzione!* Make way for the horse!"

Motorcycles, cars, pedestrians, all came to a sudden halt. As the boy guided Dorina across the street, the Chief walked alongside. "Giorgio!" he said confidingly,

"Ramalli's horses now have greater chance for being chosen."

"Why, Signore?"

"Because Doctor Celli's mare is withdrawn."

"So?"

The Chief nodded. "She suffers severe with the colic. Now only fourteen horses remain in the trials."

Giorgio felt honored that the Chief had stopped traffic for him and had called him by name. But the news was in no way startling, for who was Doctor Celli and how could an unknown mare affect his chances?

When the judges accepted Dorina and Imperiale, too, in the trial races, Giorgio felt an inward satisfaction, yet he was not surprised. He had known all along they would be chosen. They were ready. They were sound. They were, as the judges agreed, "neither too fine-boned for the cobblestone track, nor too clumsy for the perils of the course."

But when Dorina was assigned to the Contrada of the Panther and Imperiale to the Giraffe, it came as a shock that neither one hired him as fantino.

"Did I not train these horses? Do I not know their ways? Why," he implored Signor Ramalli, "why did they not choose *me*?"

Out of kindness the man gave no real answer at all. He only shrugged and said, "Man's ways are strange, Giorgio, very strange." And to lessen the blow, he added, "Perhaps, months ago they hired their fantinos."

Little Anna, however, told the truth. On the morning of the Palio she came into the stable while Giorgio was solemnly mucking out the two empty stalls. "Poor unhappy Dorina and Imperiale," she said. "They must be homesick in the strange stables of their contradas. And maybe they will bolt when the new fantinos leap on their backs."

Giorgio flushed. Even this small girl felt pity for him, and took this way of showing it. He turned his back on her, but every fiber of him was listening.

She prattled on. "I think it most foolish of the Panthers and the Giraffes to choose riders from far away."

Giorgio wondered. Did she know the real reason? "Why did they?" he blurted.

Anna stood twisting her braids, almost afraid to say. "You promise not to tell Babbo if I tell you?"

"I promise," he quickly agreed.

"Well, then," she began importantly, "to our house came some visitors. You see, it is sad, and Babbo already is sad. So you must not sadden him more. You promise?"

"Twice now I promise."

"Well, one man says to Babbo, 'Giorgio is too young for Palio battle,' and the other says, 'Giorgio is not only young, he is puny. And his hands . . .'" Anna caught her lips between her teeth and hesitated.

"Go on! Go on!"

"They say, 'His hands are . . . *girl's* hands. They cannot whack with the nerbo and hold the reins too.'"

Blood climbed hot in Giorgio's cheeks. "Girl's hands!" Was that it? He would show the Giraffe! He would show the Panther! He would show all the contradas! Because his hands were small, did this make them weak? Because he had less beard than other fantinos, did this make him green in the handling of horses? No! A thousand times no! Some boys are old before their time. "I was born old," he thought. He could never remember when he had not worked, nor when in the sweat of his work he had not dreamed of doing great things, of proving himself big for his size.

The day that was to have been all shining glory turned to ashes. In dull numbness Giorgio lived out the Palio of July second. As the sound of shields rattling and drums beating and battle cries came to him, he bridled Lubiana and rode far outside the city walls. She was not good enough for the Palio; neither was he. He rode for hours. He could almost have reached Monticello, but purposely he went the opposite way. How could he face the unasked questions of Mamma and Babbo? How could he face Emilio wearing a spennacchiera in his thatch of hair, daring his little friends to knock it off?

It was long past dark when he returned to the city. From within the walls he heard music coming toward him. The Wolves were chanting their victory song, loud in celebration.

Unable to bear the haunting sadness, he led Lubiana through the narrow side streets to her stable. Then, exhausted, he tip-toed to his room and fell across the bed. He lay there staring into the darkness, the din of the drums beating through his tired brain.

From that day on, Giorgio worked his string of horses with renewed dedication. It was the only way to hide his hurt. Men and children came in twos and threes to watch, then in knots of ten or more. He was hardly aware of them. He did not look to see if they were peasants or landowners, strangers or Sienese.

One early morning when he was working Imperiale, a new exercise boy came to Giorgio's favorite road to school his mare. He was really not a boy at all, but a small-headed, long-bodied weasel of a man, and he rode a tight rein.

Giorgio made a quick appraisal of the mare, and something within him snapped. His heart seemed to stop in its beating, then began to race wildly. The creature was an Arabian, her mantle a gleaming gray, flecked with brown. And her head was delicately shaped, with the muzzle small, and the eyes enormous and wide-set. There was no mistaking the eyes. He did not even need to think. She was, she had to be—Farfalla!

Unconsciously he slowed the pace of his mount. He thought: "She is like a piece of sculpture. Some day I will make a statue of her. And I will give it to our museum at school and there she will stand among my childish works."

All this he thought before he deigned to look at the groom who had bitted Farfalla too tightly. Should he tell the clumsy fellow you handle an Arabian differently from all others? That you ride with almost a slack rein? And the whip, does he not know it only makes creatures like her more nervous, sometimes even vicious? Where has she been since that Sunday morning at Casalino? Who owns her now? Is he kind or cruel?

Giorgio rode Imperiale alongside Farfalla, changing his pace to match hers. Then he rattled off his questions. Each one was met with glum and stolid silence.

At last the man nosed the air. "I got no time to talk to a boy with the slough of the Maremma all over him!" And he dragged out the word "boy" to put Giorgio in his place, and also to get rid of him. Then, digging his spurs into the mare's sides, he made a rude sign with his thumb, and galloped off.

Day after day the two schooled their mounts along the same road. Always the wizened groom kept his distance. It was almost as if he might be tainted by associating with someone from the Maremma. There were other roads about Siena, equally good, but the man and the boy seemed drawn to this one by some urge beyond their control, some sinister force egging them on to match their mounts and their wits.

One day the schooling gave way to a fist fight.

"Boy, go find yourself another road!" the man commanded.

And Giorgio leaned forward. "Why should *I* go?"

"Because you're a milksop; too sissy to fight!"

This was the spark that touched it off. Giorgio leaped from his mount, tied him to a sapling, caught the man's foot, swung him off Farfalla, and began punching with both fists.

The wiry groom ducked the blows, tossed Giorgio into the dirt, and would have trampled him mercilessly had not Farfalla taken this moment to fly past, her heels narrowly scraping the man's head. It was all the advantage Giorgio needed. He caught the groom off guard, sprang to his feet, and grasping the man's arms, he

pinned them tight to his sides. The groom lowered his head, butting it against Giorgio's, and at the same time twisted his shoulders, trying to wrench free. But Giorgio held fast, his arms locked tight around the lean body.

"Look!" the groom cried in mock alarm. "Farfalla escapes!"

Giorgio turned. The two animals were quietly eating the leaves of the sapling. After one well-planted blow, he freed the man in great disgust. "Get on your horse!" he cried, and watched the bowed legs scuttle off to mount Farfalla.

In this way the suspenseful days of July passed and the August Palio drew near. A week before, Imperiale developed a swelling on his left foreleg, had to be blistered, and was withdrawn from the race. But Dorina again passed the trials, and this time was assigned to the Contrada of the Porcupine. And again, no one from any contrada approached Giorgio to say, "Giorgio Terni, we earnestly desire you to be our fantino." And he could not use the reply he had rehearsed awake and asleep: "Signore, I am honored deeply to ride in the Palio for your contrada."

When the day of August the sixteenth came and the bell in the Mangia Tower began tolling, Giorgio forgot he was man-grown. With all his clothes on, even his high-laced country boots, he went to bed like a child and pulled the covers up over his head. But still he could hear the bell, sonorous and deep; could see the pageant unfold in his mind, telling the beads of history. The solemn tolling went on and on. And when he could stand the reverberations no longer, they suddenly stopped. The dead quiet that followed was even harder to bear. It meant the race was on! Giorgio saw it in all its wild and glorious beauty, heard the onlookers cheering, then roaring loud and louder until the noise filled his room. Drenched in sweat, he burrowed deeper into the covers. He wished he could suffocate and die. Unless he could be part of the Palio, he would rather be dead.

At last exhaustion took over and he fell into a jerking sleep. It was Signora Ramalli and Anna who wakened him, turning on the electric bulb. He flew out of bed, embarrassed to play the role of a sulky child.

"Giorgio," the Signora spoke in a mothering voice, "we come with the special things you like—macaroni and coffee for strength, and a good mocha torte to sweeten your bitterness." She set the tray on his table and pulled out his chair. Then she and Anna sat down on the chest to watch him eat.

Giorgio smiled his thanks. He picked up his fork and tried the macaroni, but it stuck in his throat. He tried the frosting of the torte, and to his relief it melted on his tongue.

"Better you were not there," Anna said. "Our Dorina was nearly last. Niduzza won for the Goose. But I thought a white mare, Farfalla, had won, so close were their heads."

Giorgio's spirits lifted. The cart horse of Casalino had nearly won!

"Babbo says the reason Dorina failed is not because there is weakness in her."

"Nor in her training," Signor Ramalli added, coming into the room. He sat on the edge of Giorgio's bed and sighed heavily. "By now you must know, son, that the agreements of the contradas beforehand play a vital role."

Giorgio put down his fork, listening.

"It will be enough for me to say that even the most unseasoned horse could win. Take any of the losers. Take Farfalla. In today's battle she may have been deliberately held back at the last moment. You must know," he repeated with all the force he could summon, "that sometimes there are secret arrangements between the captains of the contradas. The fantino is given orders. He *has* to lose, even when his heart cries out to win. There is no choice."

*Chapter XIII*

## THE GODDESS FORTUNA

Time in Siena is reckoned by the Palio. Trips, even important ones, are postponed until after a Palio, or made hurriedly before. In the family Bible, births and deaths are often recorded by it; this person was born on the eve of the Palio of July, 1939; that one died during the August Palio of 1880.

Giorgio, too, began counting time by the Palio. In between, he felt himself in a vacuum. There seemed no real stuff and substance to living. He remembered an incident when he was a small boy. He was watching a veterinarian standing over a sick horse, and the man had said, "This beast I do not pronounce dead; it exists in a state of suspended animation." Then with a long needle the doctor injected medicine into the horse's heart, and it began to breathe, and to live again. The Palio was a stimulant, just like that. Even the hopes dashed and the despair were easier to endure than the dull ticking of time between.

Signor Ramalli kept Giorgio on for the winter, but often on Sundays he was allowed to go to Monticello. At home one evening, with the cat purring on his shoulder and Emilio and Teria looking on, he started work on his statue of Farfalla. It was strange how he remembered everything about her, even to the length of her mane and tail. As he worked, he found himself putting a shapeless lump on her back. He pinched and pressed, adding clay here, taking it off there, until the lump began to take form.

"What!" Emilio exclaimed, his eyes round in curiosity. "What are you making there! A fantino? Is it you?"

Studying it, the mother said, "Why tear out your heart in an aching for the Palio? Some of us are meant to dress the table for the others to eat. They are blessed, too."

Giorgio managed a smile, but the longing for the Palio persisted. In the slow months that followed, he sometimes wished he had never listened to the Umbrella Man. But deep inside he knew he did not mean it; he was glad he had the next Palio to think of. The next one would be different. He would be in it, and the horse he rode would be an Arabian, almost white. And all the rest of his life the Palios would come, year after year, one wild race for glory after another.

The next Palio was different indeed. The contest really began on the road where the weasely groom and Giorgio waged their continual warfare. Grimy and sweating, Giorgio was trying one day to teach a mare to lead with either her right foreleg or her left when going into a canter. Unless she could take a curve on the correct lead, her legs might cross and she could fall, endangering herself and everyone on the course.

Farfalla, with her groom sitting smug and superior, was executing a series of perfect half-turns down the center of the road. Every time their paths crossed, the man sniped at Giorgio with a sharp insult. "Hey, you! To teach a donkey, is necessary the teacher is less donkey than the donkey. Ha! Ha!"

Giorgio usually ignored the quips and jibes, but this one cut deep because it was overheard by two important-looking men beckoning him to the side of the road. One, a dignified man with balding head, introduced himself as Signor de Santi, an attorney, and captain of the Contrada Nicchio, the Shell.

The other, towering and magnificent in his blue uniform, was Giorgio's friend, the Chief-of-the-Guards. In an easy, knowing way the Chief took hold of the mare's bridle and looked up at the boy's dirt-streaked face. He smiled as if he had heard the taunt but ignored it. "Giorgio!" he exclaimed, "we come with a message for you."

He turned to the Captain, who now cleared his throat as if he were about to address a jury. "We of the Shell," he intoned, "have sought a fantino raised in our own contrada, but," he cleared his throat again, "such a one cannot be found. Here am I, therefore, wandering over the countryside, seeking."

Giorgio was struck dumb by the importance of the two men, and embarrassed by his own appearance. Hastily, he wiped his face on his sleeve and with his fingers combed his hair.

The Captain boomed on. "Seeing you with your stained shirt and disordered hair makes me think of the words of Angelo Mentoni, who said, 'In order to make a fantino for the Palio, three requisites are needed—age, liver, and misery.' Age you have not; of your liver I know not; but misery you have—in a manner only too evident!"

Giorgio blushed, then began to shake all over in anticipation. Trees went spinning before his eyes, the sky tilted, and the men's faces swam before him as if they were under water. He knew that out of respect he should dismount, but in his dizzy excitement he might fall sprawling at their feet.

"I am of the opinion," the Captain continued, "that

you are a boy of good future and will fight earnestly to win. Unfortunately, we are not a contrada of great wealth. However, in the event of victory you will be rewarded in proportion to our limited means." He coughed apologetically. "You must realize, boy, that on our part this is a dangerous risk. Your . . . ah . . . smallness, while an advantage when riding in the provincial races, is no advantage at all on a cobblestone course where riders sit bareback."

Giorgio wanted to shout: "Capitano! Chief-of-the-Guards! I will take the risk. I will ride for no pay at all! I will pay you if I can! I will save my fare to Monticello!" Then suddenly came the remembrance of home—of the sausage hanging from the ceiling and the pieces of bread rubbed against it for flavor, and he gulped. He tried to say, "Signor de Santi, I am honored deeply to ride in the Palio for your contrada," but the words stuck in his throat.

The Captain took the silence for consent. "Good!" he said, "you shall be the fantino of the Shell for the Palio of July the second. You shall present yourself at my study on the morning when the horses are assigned." He reached up, grasping Giorgio's hand, wringing it until it hurt. Then the Chief did the same, and their eyes met in the complete understanding of one horseman for another.

For the first time in his life Giorgio galloped all the way back. He brought his mount in blowing and lathered, a thing he had never done before. Quickly he sloshed water over her. He scraped off the excess. He put a blanket on her. He walked her cool. Then he tried to

walk himself cool, up and down the Via Fontebranda, but his feet barely touched the cobblestones. He could not walk; he paced, he ran, he galloped. He felt like some god of long ago, like Mercury skimming the clouds.

That evening when Signor Ramalli heard Giorgio's news, his face lighted in pleasure. "If this honor had come to my own flesh and blood," he said, "I could not be more glad. It is honor indeed that the Captain comes to you so long before the assignment of the horses. He must consider you able to handle any mount."

Later, in the stillness of night, Giorgio wrote to his father and mother. "Mamma and Babbo," he carefully formed the letters, "to you I will dedicate my first Palio. And to Farfalla."

Not for one instant did he doubt that Farfalla would be chosen to run. Nor that in the drawing when the horses are assigned to the various contradas, the Contrada of Nicchio, the Shell, would win her. "It *has* to be," he told himself.

A month later, at the trials, Giorgio watched without breathing as Farfalla nearly took a spill at the starting rope but caught stride and finished fourth. In Giorgio's mind his arch enemy, the groom who rode her, was entirely to blame for the bad start. But even so, she was among the ten chosen.

Giorgio sighed in relief. This, he felt, was the first step toward his goal, and certain proof that he would ride her in the Palio. Was she not Bianca's successor?

Were not their life threads destined to come together?

After the trials the very air of the Piazza seemed charged with intolerable suspense. The drawing was at hand. The hour was ten-thirty, the sun striking hot on the cobblestones. Still rankling over the clumsiness of Farfalla's groom, Giorgio joined the throng gathering in front of the Palazzo Pubblico.

Everything was beginning to happen. Ten *barbarescos* or official grooms, in the brilliant costumes of their contradas, were taking their places before a raised platform. Ten trumpeters were mounting the steps, lining up at the front edge, ready to blow on their silver trumpets. The Mayor and the captains were seating themselves at a long table.

The stage was set. Two tall urns were already placed far apart on the table. Within their opaque beauty they held the fate of the drawing—in one the names of the contradas, in the other the numbers of the horses. And against the Palace wall two racks were hung, where everyone could plainly see them; they were empty, waiting for the matched names and numbers.

Seemingly the whole town was on hand, each person tense, each praying that his contrada would draw the best horse. Already the ten were rated . . . this one for speed, that one for endurance. Giorgio listened to what people were saying.

"Ah, Belfiore is a veteran of many Palios. She knows those sharp curves like the corners of her stall!"

"Oh, ho! Do not overlook Ravi, the little black gelding."

"If Bruco, the Caterpillar, does not draw a good horse," said a man with a cracked voice, "I will go to the country."

"Then go!" The jeers were ribald. "In thirty years your Bruco does not win the Palio."

"Si, si," taunted a gleeful young voice. "Bruco wears the grandmother's cap." And everyone took up the singing cry: "Bruco wears the grandmother's cap! Bruco wears the grandmother's cap!"

It was stilled only by the trumpeters blasting forth on their silver horns. Then a hushed silence as two small pages stepped forward to the center of the stage. In military precision they turned smartly on their heels. One marched to the urn at the right end of the table, and the other to the urn at the left. While everyone watched, breathless, they took from each urn a wooden capsule and with a deep bow presented it to the Mayor.

The Mayor's hands shook violently as he opened the first capsule, unrolled a white slip of paper, and held it high for the crowd to see.

"Number six!" Every voice roared as one voice.

Quick as a wink, a man scrambled up a ladder and slid a number 6 into the top space of one rack.

Giorgio glanced into the corral nearby, where the mare Belfiore wore a number 6 beneath her ear.

The crowd went wild. "Give us Belfiore!" they cried. "Give us Belfiore!"

Then silence clamped down as the Mayor opened the second capsule and held up the paper. Those nearby read it, and almost before their lips formed the name, the man on the ladder slid the board marked "Porcupine" into the rack beside number six.

The Porcupines were beside themselves with joy. "Already we have won!" they shouted.

Giorgio felt a tightening of his chest. He began to know fear. Why had he been so sure the Nicchio would draw Farfalla? With each capsule opened, fresh beads of sweat rolled down his back. He could feel his shirt cling damply to him. He listened to the pairing in an agony of suspense.

"Ravi to the Caterpillar."

"Mitzi to the Goose."

"Saró non saró to the Tower."

"Anita to the Panther."

"Goia to the Snail."

"Lirio to the Wave."

"Tarantella to the Turtle."

"Fontegiusta to the Unicorn."

Only two contradas left; only two horses left! And now the last spaces in the racks filling in, irrevocably:

"Farfalla to the Forest."

"Turbolento to Nicchio, the Shell."

Giorgio was too stunned to move. In minutes, the Goddess Fortuna had knocked down his hopes as if they were toy blocks. He watched the members of the Forest lead Farfalla away to their stable. And he let the people of the Shell push him along with them to surround the dark bay, Turbolento. He was glad for the jostling crowd, and the deafening noise—the happy shrieks, and the wails of the disappointed ones. He wanted to wail, too, but Captain de Santi had turned to him, his face alight with joy. Above the din he introduced four strapping young men.

"Your bodyguard," he shouted. "They will protect you from harm, and us from interference. Wherever you go, from one dawn to the next, they will be with you."

There was a look so desolate on the boy's face that the Captain gripped his shoulder. "Have you nothing to say? Nothing at all? Are you not happy?"

Numb, drenched in misery, Giorgio heard his long-rehearsed speech come out at last: "Capitano, I am honored deeply to ride for your contrada."

*Chapter XIV*

## AT THE CURVE OF SAN MARTINO

In spite of his disappointment, Giorgio's spirits began to rise with each passing hour. Even if he could not ride Farfalla in the Palio, he was no longer an outcast. He was a participant! And for a week at least he would be free of the weasel of a groom with his sly grin and razor tongue.

That same day of the drawing, and for three successive days, the rehearsal races were held. They were called *Provas,* but Giorgio failed to see that they proved anything.

In the first one he was eager to make a good showing

for the Shell, and he lifted Turbolento up over the starting rope before it actually touched the track. In fact, he was well in the lead when he noticed that none of the other fantinos were urging their mounts. They made a great to-do with flapping elbows and wild yelling, but anyone could see they were intent on concealing their mounts' true ability.

Giorgio followed their cue. Besides, after the first spurt, he sensed that he might have trouble with Turbolento. Although not new to racing, the horse was accustomed to the tracks in the provinces. The races there were run counterclockwise, while here in the Piazza del Campo the running went clockwise. It would take patient control of Turbolento's speed and of his leads to prevent his switching at the turns. Before Giorgio had gone once around the Piazza, he understood the real purpose of the Prova. Horses and riders had to get acquainted three ways—with each other, with the dangerous slopes and curves, and with the opposite way of running. No wonder the rehearsal races were neither battle nor competition!

During the days of the Provas, Giorgio felt as if he had the all-seeing eyes of a horse. Besides watching Turbolento's every move, he managed to see what was happening to Farfalla, whether she was ahead of him or behind. Her fantino, Ivan-the-Terrible, went around the curves flapping his wings like a bird. Twice he flew off into space. Luckily, Farfalla was not hurt by entangling reins or bumps from other horses. Giorgio remembered later that he had noticed Ivan was unhurt only after he had made sure about Farfalla!

"Which horse is it you ride?" an elderly man of the Forest whispered to Giorgio after the third Prova. "Is it your Turbolento, or is it our Farfalla?" And he winked and nudged him in the ribs as if he wished the boy could be their fantino.

Quickly Giorgio's bodyguards closed in, wondering if the man were making some secret offer. But they might have saved themselves the trouble, for neither Turbolento nor Giorgio was considered strong enough to win—or to help anyone else to win.

Despite his watchfulness, Giorgio failed to see the crippling accident that happened to Farfalla in the last Prova on the very morning of the Palio. Between the curves of San Martino and the Casato, the horses of the Panther and the Unicorn were having a private race of their own. As Farfalla tried to pass, a hoof lashed out and hit her a sharp blow, almost severing the cartilage of her left hind foot. Ivan-the-Terrible managed to stay on, and let her finish the race limping heavily.

Moments later Giorgio passed her in a narrow lane as she was being led back to her stable. He turned to look at her bleeding heel. "The devil pursues her!" he said to his guards. Then his eyes blazed with a sudden thought. "They won't race her; they *can't* race her this afternoon in the Palio!" he cried out.

"But they got to!" the young men answered in chorus, and they turned on him in a torrent of explanation.

"It is a law from year seventeen hundred," the Number One guard said. "If an animal is lamed or dies in a Prova, it is not permitted to replace him."

Another guard broke in excitedly. "Why, I myself saw one killed in a Prova, and the contrada remained horseless."

"I too saw it!" the first one said. "And in the parade before the race the long black tail and the severed hoof of the dead one were carried on a platter of silver."

Now thoroughly roused, the guards were irrepressible. "And the flags of that contrada were tightly furled in mourning and even the strongest men wept like small children and cried aloud."

Giorgio felt his stomach turn over. Almost pleading, he looked from face to face. "But Farfalla is crippled! There could be a stumble, a fatal . . ."

"Then it will be her time to die," the Number One bodyguard said flatly. "She too is only mortal." There was no coldness in his voice. He was merely repeating words said to him long ago.

Giorgio tried to shut out thoughts of Farfalla. He made his mind go forward. He began counting. Three hours until the blessing of the horses in the churches of their contradas. Then the long historical parade, and at last, at sundown, the Palio!

He went with Turbolento into the stable of the Shell and watched the barbaresco go to work, sponging him off, making him comfortable and cool with especial attention to his head, eyes, and nostrils. Giorgio stood by as long as he could. Then from sheer habit he fell to his knees and hand-rubbed Turbolento's legs. Unconsciously he worked for a long time on the left hind, as if in some remote way he were helping Farfalla.

Giorgio usually had the mind of a camera. Events registered sharply with him. But that afternoon, during the long parade in which he wore the martial costume of the Middle Ages and rode a heavy warhorse, he felt himself an actor in a play, an actor who did not know his part. He was bewildered by the vast sea of faces in the center of the Piazza, and the kaleidoscope of color in costumes and flags, and the drums beating out a somber rhythm. Through it all he rode woodenly, like a toy soldier.

But with the explosion of the bomb announcing the race, he became all awareness again. With every fiber he heard the starter call out the horses in order.

"Number one, Caterpillar!"

"Number two, Shell!"

"Number three, Forest!" That was Farfalla. Ignoring her injury, she walked briskly to the starting rope. Giorgio reminded himself that of course the doctors had deadened her pain.

As the horses moved to their positions, Giorgio felt his breath coming fast. Turbolento and Farfalla were side by side. "Is it some omen," he asked himself, "that brings us together?"

The starter's voice blared on: "Number four, Tower . . . Number five, Snail . . . Number six, Wave . . . Number seven, Panther . . . Number eight, Goose . . . Number nine, Turtle!"

Now nine horses in line—pawing, dancing, heads pulling to go. And nine fantinos with faces taut, reins taut, waiting for the number ten horse. Not until he is called to the rope can the race begin.

"Number ten, Unicorn!" the strident voice of the starter fills the Piazza.

Head lowered like a bull charging, the number ten horse gallops up, almost touches the rope. The starter springs it. It snakes free. Ten horses, as one, leap over it!

Giorgio's fingers tighten hard around the nerbo. If he takes the lead, he will not need it. He arrows Turbolento out in front, sets the pace.

Forty thousand throats cry *"Forza! Forza!"* as the bunched leaders pass the Fonte Gaia, pass the Casino of the Nobles, pass the scaffold where the judges sit. Now they are thundering toward the death curve of San Martino.

Behind him Giorgio hears the nerbos strike hollow against horseflesh and sharp against steel helmets, but he is still in the lead, free of the bludgeoning.

Out of the tail of his eye he sees the Wave, the Goose, the Panther fighting it out, and behind them Ivan-the-Terrible trying to drive Farfalla through. In the split second of his looking, a fantino catapults into the air like a rag doll shot from a cannon. It must be Ivan! It *is* Ivan! Farfalla is staggering on by herself. All this Giorgio senses rather than sees. He is at the curve now. Turbolento is leaning at a crazy angle; he seems to be tiring, faltering.

From every balcony and window, from all over the Piazza, the people of the Shell are shouting to Giorgio: "The nerbo! The nerbo! Use the nerbo on him!"

Giorgio feels icy terror. Turbolento is trying to wheel, to run the wrong way of the track. His left foreleg crosses his right. It is rooted! The pack is passing him! From both sides nerbos are raining blows on him, on Giorgio, beating them out of the way.

Giorgio lifts the horse's head, tries to get the weight on his hocks, but it is too late! Turbolento freezes, then buckles. His scream joins the shrieks of the crowd as he somersaults and slides across the track. Giorgio is pitched into the air, and hits with a thud on his back.

Hoofs go thundering past while he lies writhing, gasping, the wind knocked out of his body. As in a trance he sees the white-coated veterinarian rush out on the track. He hears the crack of the bullet that ends Turbolento's life, and sees the limping form of Farfalla come within an arm's length of the smoking pistol.

His heart beats thickly. He is suddenly afraid. A soundless prayer escapes his lips.

"Not her, too! O Holy Mother, not her! Not her!"

*Chapter XV*

## THE ODD PIECES AGAIN

He was still gulping for air, but he had to move before the horses came around again. He felt a pair of strong hands grasping his upper arms, helping to lift him. Feeling less hurt than humiliated, he pulled away. It was not his body that needed help. He made his knees bend one at a time, and he pushed himself up. And he got to his feet under his own power and as the horses whirled past, he went tottering alongside, clinging to the upright mattresses that lined the curve.

With his sleeve he wiped the sweat and a streak of blood from his face and he sucked air enough to walk head up. But the pain of remembered sounds and sights bore down on him—the sharp crack of the bullet, the instantaneous thud, the dribble of crimson, the crazed scream cut short. Then the whole world was a spinning blackness. What had happened afterward?

All about him a solid pack of humanity was streaming onto the track. The race was over! Voices came at him like cross winds, some shouting "Bravo!" and some crying in strange foreign tongues. He was sucked along with the crowd, stumbling, shuffling, pulled into their meshes like a fish into a net. Over and above the shouting came wild, deafening cheers, beating out the syllables:

"*Tar-tu-ca!*"

"*Tar-tu-ca!*"

And so he knew that the Contrada of the Turtle had won. And he yelled, too, but he did not know what he yelled. He had to yell to keep from fainting, to keep from crying.

Two of his bodyguards got through the crowd to him, linked their arms in his, supporting him, buoying him along, questioning in his ear.

"How do you feel?"

"You all right?"

His head nodded "yes" but all of him felt numbed, disgraced. And his legs trembled as if at any moment they might splay and split apart. Through the shouting and joyful singing, he could hear remembered voices mocking:

"Hey, you runt of Monticello!"

"You, with the slough of the Maremma all over you!"

"Girl's hands . . . girl's hands . . . girl's hands . . ."

The words jumbled in his dizziness, and he staggered along, feeling himself littler and weaker than ever, like some fragile moth battering its wings against the walls of the centuries. He knew now what the Umbrella Man meant. The Palio was indestructible. Men could beat their fists against it. Horses and fantinos could die for it, but it would remain forever the supreme challenge.

He wanted to be alone in his agony. His guards understood, and let him go. As he went zigzagging through the crowd, he pressed his palms hard against his ears, trying to shut out the singing, and the drums beating, and the inner voices accusing. At last he stood panting before the door of Turbolento's stable.

He rang the bell, summoning the barbaresco. He knocked. No one came.

A couple walked by, arm in arm, unmindful of him. He might have been a cat scratching to be let in. He tried the latch. The door was open! He lurched into the dark emptiness. The barbaresco was not there. No one was on guard. No one was needed. He closed the door behind him, and his shaking hands locked it. The light from a street candle came in the high barred window, threw a splash of yellow on the strawed bed of Turbolento. It was freshly made, awaiting a possible victor.

Alone in the stable, with only the faraway sounds of rejoicing, Giorgio fell face down in the straw. "Mammina! Mammina!" he sobbed, and the tears so long inheld were unloosed. As he cried himself out, the sea of taunting faces melted away, and in their stead his mother's face appeared, trying to soothe him, to comfort him. "Giorgio, Giorgio, Giorgio," she called.

The next day millions of people were reading newspaper accounts of the Palio. Sports writers from Rome, from Florence, from Milan called it "The Race of the Broken Heart." They referred not to the death of Turbolento. That was gallant. For a horse to be killed on the field, like a soldier in battle, was beautiful. But the injury to Farfalla's leg, they said, was not only painful to her and perilous to all, but to watch her hobbling three times around the course to the very end was heartbreaking. Better she, too, had been killed.

Thus, in a few paragraphs, the race passed into history. For weeks, however, the fate of Farfalla was tossed about like a frail boat in a storm. One doctor gave her an even chance of going sound again. Another spoke frankly to her owner as father to son.

"Celli," he said, "you are a man most benevolent, but that poor mare is suffering, and time will not lessen her pain." He shook his head in sympathy. "I suggest you put her down, and the sooner it is done, the better."

Unwilling to be convinced, Doctor Celli called in

a third veterinarian, a gnomelike creature with a short clipped mustache and a short clipped way of speaking. After examining Farfalla, who was biting at her manger, he made his pronouncement: "This Palio will be her last. I would at once put an end to her sufferings. What pleasure in this life does she have?"

For hours after the veterinarian had gone, Doctor Celli paced to and fro in the room where he kept his guns and hunting trophies. It was difficult to listen to one's heart and mind at the same time. As a banker he was a careful man, reasoning always with his pocketbook. A sick horse was a luxury he could ill afford. If the best doctors were ready to sign her death warrant, who was he to say, "No, this I will not do!" Yet he could not help wavering.

Perhaps, he mused, someone else would have more time to give her, more time to look in on her during the day instead of only at sunup and sundown. Would Signor Busisi know of someone? A talk with the old and wise man might be of help.

Feeling somewhat lifted in his heart, Doctor Celli went to his garage, backed out his car, and sped toward Siena. He would lay the facts in the palm of his friend and ask for a plain answer.

Within the half hour the door to the house of Busisi was opening wide and the sad, kindly face of the Signore was smiling in welcome.

"Buona sera, Celli. Come in! Come in!" The old

man led the way to the dining table and pulled out a chair. "Enjoy with me the simple pleasure of food and drink. I am alone. My wife has gone to the church. Let us eat first. Then we talk of Farfalla."

There was a bottle of good red wine on the table and a nice assortment of cheeses. Signor Busisi fixed a plate of them for his guest. Without any heart for it, Doctor Celli took a small bite of the gorgonzola.

The old man remonstrated. "Celli, can you only nibble like the mouse? Eat with gusto!"

"If I eat now, Signore, the food sits heavy in my stomach. I want only to talk." He pushed his plate aside. "Already I have summoned three veterinarians for Farfalla."

"And their verdict?"

"Two advise putting her down. At once."

"You have decided?"

"No. My thoughts seesaw—first one way, then the other. You observed her in the Palio, Signore. What would you say if she were now fretting in your stable instead of in mine?"

Signor Busisi's face was grave, deeply concerned. He made a steeple of his fingertips and looked under them as if he hunted there for the answer. "Mortals are quick to destroy," he said at last. Already he was ill of a heart condition, and being on the edge of death himself seemed to give him a wisdom beyond the common man. "It takes eleven months and five days for a horse to be born into this world," he said with a faraway look. "Why do we not give the mare the same number of months and days before we sentence her to die? Perhaps in that time she will prove her destiny."

There was a long silence between them. The old man got up, paced the room thoughtfully, then stood before the window. A blood-red sun was sinking behind the city wall. With his back to Doctor Celli he said, "You are not the first to come to me today concerning the fate of Farfalla."

"So? Who else?"

"The Chief-of-the-Town-Guards. You know him?"

"Si, si. The Chief is a man most compassionate. I once saw him on a cold, bitter day restore the fallen blanket to an old bony horse."

"But the Chief came only as agent."

"Agent?"

Signor Busisi nodded.

"Agent for whom?"

"For two tradesmen from Seggiano."

"But what could *they* want with Farfalla?"

"In their hands she would certainly come to a pitiful end. But . . ." Signor Busisi came back to the table; he seemed quite out of breath.

"But what?"

"I detected something in the face of the Chief," the Signore went on. "At first it was only a flicker, then it burst into flame, bright as the morning sun. You see, he had been charged to buy Farfalla, but suddenly the truth struck him. He did not want to forward the mare to Seggiano. He wanted to keep her for himself."

Doctor Celli sat on the very edge of his chair. "What did you tell him?"

"I told him what I once told you."

"You mean about life being a puzzle with odd-shaped pieces?"

The old man threw back his head and laughed. "My boy, you have a remarkable memory. And I told him also what sweet frenzy it would be for him in next year's Palio to watch two horses—his own and that of his contrada."

Doctor Celli smiled. In the hands of the Chief, Farfalla would be treated well. She might live to race again. She might even . . .

Signor Busisi broke into his reverie. "I must tell you," he said, "the Chief's money at present is low, but he is soon expecting payment on an old transaction, and my advice, Celli, is for you to wait until he comes to you, ready to buy. Remember this, my friend, a gift horse seldom is prized."

"I will wait! Gladly! Farfalla meanwhile can rest at my country place, and my tenant farmer will see to her needs." With a deep sigh of relief he stood up and raised his glass in a toast. "May the pieces fit again!"

Already the heaviness was lifted from his heart.

*Chapter XVI*

## THE RABBIT'S FOOT AND THE HORN

The second Palio of 1953 was bloodless, but again it fell short of Giorgio's dreams. Not until the last moment did any contrada ask him to ride. Then on a cold-blooded horse he raced for the Panthers. A flashy bay won for the Forest, but of course Farfalla was not there. Things might have been different, he thought, if he had had the right mount. He wondered what had become of her, if she would ever race again.

On a morning soon afterward, Giorgio set out quite early for the weekly market held in the Piazza del Campo.

He was leaving for Monticello that selfsame day, but first he had a purchase to make. He planned to walk all the way home to save for his mother the few lire he had left from his year in Siena. And since it was the season of the rains, he would need either a raincoat or an umbrella. A raincoat would make him look more like a successful fantino, but it would cost 5,000 lire, and for that sum he could buy four umbrellas! Besides, he had ruined his only satchel with blistering liniments and blue gentian for his horses, and he would need a carryall for his clothes. By rolling them into small, bread-size bundles he could pack them between the ribs of an umbrella. And so, for one price, he would have a traveling bag and a canopy against the rain.

As he trudged the steep hill of Via Fontebranda, he felt cross-arrows of sadness and gladness. The sadness was for his performance in the Palios. Two contradas had believed in him and he had failed them, miserably. He had failed his family, and himself, too. Even Signor Ramalli needed him no more; he was selling his horses and would not start up his stable again until spring, if then.

So now, defeated and discouraged, Giorgio was going back home where he belonged. That was the wonderful thing about Home. It waited patiently for you to come back, hero or failure. In his mind's eye he was already there, his mother singing as she whisked an egg for their soup; his father contentedly blowing smoke rings; the children poking their fingers through them. And pervading the whole house was the comforting, all-is-well feeling, as if downy wings were spread wide and all who came within were safe.

He was deep in these thoughts as he joined the procession of men with their baskets and women with their market bags. He decided not to make his purchase right away, but to move through the crowd, enjoying the sights and sounds. He had to laugh at a bearded old man in an ankle-length coat who picked up a lady's mirror and a goose quill from a counter of trinkets and trifles. Unmindful of anyone else, he studied his long yellow teeth in the mirror, picked them clean with the goose quill, and tossed both articles back on the table. Enraged, the man behind the counter promptly smashed the mirror on the cobblestones. "You miser! You horse's teeth!" he called out. "For you this means worst luck."

Giorgio walked on, still laughing. Life was fun, after all. He stopped at another stand, fascinated by a hawker of handkerchiefs. The man was wrapping one after another about his fist until the bundle grew big as a pumpkin. He kept his audience in an uproar as he wound and wound the white squares. "Peoples!" he shouted. "A thousand uses they have! To clean the rifle. To strain the jelly. To substitute for the diaper. To blow the nose, even great one like Pinocchio's. Now, who wants whole bundle for only two hundred lire. Who wants?"

Hands went up in coveys, like birds flushed from a

hedgerow. And the money poured in. Giorgio could not help wondering if men like this—men who could make so much money and who could make people laugh, too—did they have worries inside them?

He went on, through the maze of hardware and pink petticoats and flower stalls, and the stalls with bright-colored fish and tiny talking birds. He bought two fish to give to Anna, and a new belt for himself. At last he came to the umbrellas. Under a bright purple awning they were hanging down like a stumpy green fringe.

The man selling them was bent double, counting shiny lire from his pocket into a copper pitcher on the ground. All Giorgio could see of him was the bright green patch on the seat of his trousers. It was the same green as the umbrellas!

When the man stopped a moment in his counting to peer around for customers, Giorgio nearly dropped his fish.

"Uncle Marco!" he shouted. "Uncle Marco!"

With a clanking jangle the remaining money fell into the pitcher uncounted. The man spun around, at the same time pushing back his feathered hat and squinting his eyes to make sure. Then he leaped over the pitcher, grabbed Giorgio by the shoulders, and bellowed for all the world to hear. "Giorgio! Giorgio Terni!" Fiercely, fondly, he embraced the boy, kissing him man-fashion, first on one cheek, then the other.

A little crowd began gathering and Uncle Marco

smiled beatifically at the ready-made audience. "Signori!" he announced, "I wouldn't believe mine eyes. Behold the little runt from Monticello!" He spoke with reverence, with ecstasy. There were tears in his eyes.

"This brave young fantino," he explained, "is more Sienese than the Sienese! Some day he will conquer curve of San Martino. You listen to your Umbrella Man! This boy will be a fantino *formidabile*! The Palio . . . he will win it!"

Red-faced, Giorgio pulled at Uncle Marco's sleeve. "Please, Uncle, please! I come to buy the umbrella. An oiled-cloth one, because they are cheaper. You see," he stammered, "today I go home to Monticello."

Uncle Marco slapped his thigh and laughed until the tears streaked down the furrows of his cheeks.

Giorgio grew angry. Was this a time to laugh? Had the Umbrella Man gone daft?

"Ah, the sadness so sweet! So joyous!" he sighed, making no sense whatsoever. A few bystanders nodded, as if they knew a sweet sadness, too. One woman began sobbing softly.

Giorgio tried to back away, but Uncle Marco lifted him bodily off his feet, giving him a bear hug, almost crushing him in happy excitement.

"Put me *down*! Put me *down*! You spill my fish!"

Uncle Marco set him down as if he were a child. "You listen to me," he said. "I foresee . . ." He let the sentence dangle teasingly in midair. Then to heighten the suspense he whispered in a stage voice directly into Giorgio's ear. But first he examined the ear, marveling at its smallness. "I foresee," he said prophetically, "to Monticello you do not go."

"Oh, but I do! This very morning I go."

"Ho, ho! Listen to him! So little faith has he."

Putting his arm around Giorgio, he faced the audience, sighing deep, as if he could hold the suspense no longer. "Someone," he pronounced, "someone *multo importante* wishes Giorgio to see. No less than the Chief-of-the-Town-Guards! Himself, the Chief!"

The crowd was enjoying the show, old men clicking their teeth, little boys nudging one another in envy.

"He wishes to see *me*?" Giorgio asked in disbelief.

"Si, si. He tries everywhere to find Giorgio Terni. First he goes to the Ramallis'; you not there. They say to him : 'Giorgio, he went to market to buy the raincoat, or maybe the umbrella.' So the Chief comes at once to me.

"'Where is Giorgio Terni?' he asks. 'You have seen him, yes?' 'No, no,' I have to say. 'Him I have not seen in long, long time.' He says, 'Giorgio will come.' 'For certain?' I ask. 'For certain,' he says."

Uncle Marco licked his lips and beamed, first upon Giorgio and then upon the audience. "So now everything is arranged. You, Giorgio Terni, must come here to Il Campo tonight at the hour of ten." He pointed across the Piazza. "Over there at the street café by the Fonte Gaia will be the Chief. He will await you. So now the umbrella you do not need. Instead . . ."

He rummaged in his pockets and pulled out a slender red horn made from sea coral. It shone brightly in his calloused hand. "Anciently," he said, crinkling his eyes until they were slits, "Roman gladiators carry this horn for best luck."

He doffed his hat and bowed as if he were conferring a knighthood. "I make a present to you, Giorgio." He held it dangling on its string before the boy, who returned bow for bow but made no comment. He could see Uncle Marco had more to say.

"And for extra good luck, here is also a small rabbit's foot. An American lady give it me for a favor. Now I give to you." He pressed both into Giorgio's hands and smiled exultantly.

*Chapter XVII*

GAUDENZIA, JOY OF LIVING

Ten o'clock seemed years away. To hurry the time, Giorgio went to the public bath and gave himself a good scrubbing. He worked hard on the labyrinthian creases in his ears. Perhaps Uncle Marco had examined them for a reason.

At supper back at the Ramallis' home he ate his macaroni in a trance, almost forgetting to say *"Buon appetito"* beforehand. There was chocolate and strawberry ice cream for dessert, served in special honor of his departure. Absentmindedly, he mashed and melted the two colors together, toying rather than tasting.

"Is something wrong with the ice cream?" Signora Ramalli asked in concern.

For answer Giorgio quickly shoved a spoonful into his mouth. How could he explain his excitement when perhaps it would amount to nothing at all?

After supper Anna wheedled him into a game of dominoes, but his eye was on the clock more than on the counters. When at last it was time to go, he grabbed his jacket and tore down the stairs and out into the street. He ran swiftly at first; then as the lane twisted and steepened, he had to slow to a walk. Someone had forgotten to take a parrot inside. The cage hung on a balcony and its occupant screamed and scolded Giorgio as if he were to blame.

On ordinary evenings he would have talked back, but tonight nothing could delay him. He did not even peer into the cobbler's shop for memory's sake, nor into the public laundry. Nor did he stop to look through the gates to the great houses.

Tonight he flew by his landmarks as he climbed the Via Fontebranda, crossed the busy Via di Città and came out at last into the fairyland of Il Campo. He caught his breath at the contrast from the morning market. The jumbled confusion of flapping blankets and spreads and the splashing colors of fruits and vegetables, and the hawkers screaming—all this was gone. The Piazza was a shell of emptiness. High up in the palace windows the winking lights seemed faraway planets, but in the circle of shops below they burned steady and close together like a necklace of fire opals.

The night was softly warm. A score of small round tables had been set out in front of the café near the Fonte Gaia. Most of them were occupied. Giorgio thought he recognized some of the people from Uncle Marco's audience. He stood facing across the vast square to the canyon of the street where the Chief lived. It was black as a mousehole. Like a cat, Giorgio watched it, never taking his eyes away. It was magic how the Chief came, as if the very looking had pulled him out of the darkness. At first he was only a tall block of white. Then gradually the block developed two legs, and with lithe grace they were advancing across the square, directly toward Giorgio.

When the two met, the Chief purposely stood on the down-slope so that he and Giorgio were more nearly the same height. Then he glanced up at the Mangia Tower. The lone hand on the clock pointed almost to the hour. He smiled in approval.

"We meet early, no?"

Giorgio nodded, too breathless to speak.

"Come, my boy," the Chief said. "See that little table apart from the others? There the long-eared folk won't hear us."

A waiter arrived at the table simultaneously. "Buona sera," he bowed. Then he wiped the chair where the Chief would sit, and gave the table a thorough cleaning.

"Now then." He arched his eyebrows, awaiting the order. "Would you like a chocolate? An ice cream? Or a coffee, perhaps?"

"What will you have, Giorgio?" the Chief inquired.

"I will take a coffee, if you please."

"We will each take the same, waiter."

There was no talk at all before the coffees arrived. Somewhere from the heights of a palace window came a string of staccato notes, clear and strong. It was flute music, the "March of the Palio."

Giorgio wiped the anxious moisture from his palms. A distant church bell chimed the hour. The time had come! And with it the two steaming cups.

"Sugar?" The waiter held the bowl first for the Chief, then set it down in front of Giorgio. Two spoonfuls went into each tiny cup, and both the man and the boy stirred vigorously, as if they had no other thought on their minds. In unison, too, they sipped the sweet bitterness.

At last the Chief looked directly at Giorgio. "Well, boy? Did you go today to the Street Market?"

"Si, si."

"Did you buy the umbrella?"

"No, Signore." Giorgio hesitated. "You see, Uncle Marco is my very good friend. He said the umbrella now is not needed. Instead, he gave me, for luck, a coral horn and a rabbit's foot."

A smile crossed the Chief's lips. "I will start from the first." He set down his cup. "Now then! Two tradesmen

from Seggiano have engaged me to purchase for them the mare, Farfalla."

Giorgio drew in a quick breath. Why did the very mention of her name give him a shock?

"They have commissioned me," the Chief went on, "to make the purchase from Doctor Celli and to forward the mare to Seggiano."

"But why? Is it for the racing?"

The Chief shook his head sadly. "I prefer not to think of her fate. Those men are traders in all manner of beasts."

"Could you . . ." Giorgio's mind darted ahead. He grew startled at his own daring. "Please, Signore, could you not buy the mare yourself?"

For a moment there was stony silence. Then in a

voice cold and stern, the Chief asked, "Who told you to say this? Signor Busisi? Doctor Celli?"

"Oh no, Signore."

"Are you certain?"

"I am certain."

The big man relaxed, and his face broke into a pleased grin. "Good! A boy who can read a man's mind can also read a horse's." Then he leaned forward, punctuating his words with excited gestures. "Already have I gone to Signor Busisi. I tell him I am commissioned to buy the mare, but in my heart I hide the secret hope of keeping her."

Giorgio barely managed to get the next words out. "Is all settled?"

"No, no. Nothing is settled! With her what would I

do? Where would I keep her? Who would exercise her? I have nobody to do this. Besides, she has the nervous malady."

Giorgio's mouth went dry. He could not speak. He took a gulp of coffee, but still no words came.

The Chief was using both hands now; his words ringing sharp and clear. "In spite that she did not reach expectation, in spite that she is tortured by the bad leg and the nervous tic, the daughter of Sans Souci deserves better than to be put down."

Suddenly the boy found his voice. "Oh, I believe it, too! I believe!"

"The money to buy her—that I now have."

Giorgio's heart raced. He thought he had the answer. He knew it was the answer. "I . . . I will train her!" he gasped.

There was no reply. Only the flute piping in the palace window.

Giorgio leaped to his feet, almost upsetting his chair. "Do not worry about the stable," he said. "In the Maremma I can winter her. Babbo has a very nice barn. Nobody lives there, nobody but little Pippa, our donkey."

Still no reply.

Giorgio persisted. "Signore! I myself can ride her to Monticello. At once!"

The Chief pursed his lips, thinking. There was worry in his face as he mulled over the proposal. He had asked expressly for this meeting, had hoped earnestly that Giorgio would have the same desire to rescue the mare. But now he was appalled by the depth of the boy's emotion. He studied the slight figure, the young face so full of eager determination. What if the mare were beyond help? Was the boy's faith too high a price to pay? What would happen to him if he failed?

Their eyes met and held. Giorgio put out his hand and suddenly the Chief reached across the table and took it in a clasp so strong it seemed as if some unseen force were bringing them together. For a moment they both fell silent, tasting their dreams. Giorgio was living his day of triumph. He saw the Palio square alive with people, and heard voices crying the names of their contradas, but mostly they were screaming to a white mare, winging her in.

Still handfast, the Chief cried, *"Forza! Forza!"*

The waiter came running. "You call me?"

"No, no," the Chief laughed heartily. "We are in the Palio."

The waiter nodded in complete understanding. There was nothing surprising in this.

"Giorgio!" The Chief spoke now in whispered confidence. "No wonder Farfalla fails. Who wants 'butterfly' for horse? We change her name! I am a man very earthy. For me, *Gaudenzia* is the name I favor. It is strong like marching music. Gau-den-zia," he repeated softly, lingering over each syllable. *"Joy-of-living*. You like?"

"I like!"

The Chief squared his shoulders. "From this very moment," he said, "the destiny of the mare changes. She will get a new name, a new life!"

"Gau-den-zia, Gaudenzia." Slowly Giorgio tested it on his tongue. The happiness was almost beyond bearing.

"That Uncle Marco," chuckled the Chief, "did he not save you the price of the umbrella? Who could hold the umbrella on horseback? It is only for sultan of the desert, not for warrior of the Palio!" He threw back his head, laughing as light-heartedly as a boy, and the flutter of notes from the palace window echoed their happiness.

*Chapter XVIII*

BACK HOME TO THE MAREMMA

The next morning broke clear and cool, and Giorgio set out before sunup for Doctor Celli's villa. He carried only a small parcel containing his clothes, which were wrapped about a chunk of bread and a salami. If Gaudenzia was fit to travel, he would make her load as light as possible.

The shadowed road was still cool from the night, and the birds only beginning to sing. Giorgio whistled as he strode along, and the notes came so light and fast he could hardly keep up with them. The song he whistled was about the common road to glory, and there was such a bursting in his chest that he half ran the shadowy climbing way to the villa on the hilltop.

The sun was less than an hour high when he stood at Doctor Celli's door, completely out of breath. "Suppose," he suddenly thought, "the doctor is a late riser! Suppose word has not reached him that I am coming and he is off hunting rabbits in the hills. Suppose the weasely groom is in charge!"

But before Giorgio could pick up the brass knocker, a beautiful shiny one made in the image of a unicorn, the door opened wide and Doctor Celli, with a dog at his heels, stepped outside.

"Buon giorno," he smiled in welcome. "Your whistling and the barking of my hound announced you well ahead of time. Before I take you to the mare, I have some things to explain." He led the way to an ornamental bench in the midst of a rose garden, and motioned Giorgio to sit beside him. The red-eyed hound nosed the boy appraisingly, then flopped at his feet.

Doctor Celli began, choosing his words carefully. "To you, I believe I can talk as man to man."

Giorgio felt a stab of uneasiness at the tone of voice. He reached down and scratched the dog's head, trying not to show concern.

"I doubt the mare is fit for travel," the doctor went on. "The hurt tendon still gives her much discomfort. Maybe in a month or two she will be ready. And if, in the meanwhile, you wish to stay here and work in the grape harvest, I would be pleased."

"A month or two!" Giorgio stared at the man, unbelieving.

Doctor Celli got to his feet and touched Giorgio on the shoulder. "Follow me," he said, and he walked down the path to a cluster of outbuildings. "I will show you where she is stabled. I have no groom now, so her bed may be soiled and her white coat stained." And in the same breath he added, "Poor beast, it was an evil bump she had in the Prova. The cartilage above the hoof is badly damaged, and the nervous tic tortures her. But of these maladies you are already aware."

He turned to smile at Giorgio as they came to a halt before the closed door of a narrow stone building. He made no move to open it. "Sometimes with strangers she is quite savage," he explained. "Therefore, I think it imperative that you establish at once who is master.

Perhaps," he questioned, "perhaps you wish to go in alone?"

Giorgio looked at the forbidding, heavy door. He drew a deep breath, hesitated, then lifted the latch and pushed. The creaking of the hinges sent Farfalla rearing to the rafters. Quietly Giorgio stepped inside and closed the door. He stood transfixed at the change in her—the ribs showing, the mantle harsh. Her stall was big enough, but lit by only one window, too high for looking out. It smelled of cold earth and hay and dung. All this he sensed in some faraway place in his mind. He had never before been alone with the mare, and he stood motionless, making no sound.

She too was electric with curiosity, pulling in the scent of him, blowing it out with a rattling snort.

"I am here," the boy said in a quiet tone. "It's only me."

The mare's head jerked high, her nostrils flared red, her ears flattened. "Stay back!" she warned. Fear was strong in her, but spirit, too. When Giorgio did not retreat, she wheeled about, took aim, and like a cat ready to spring, she gathered herself for a mighty kick. In the split second before her heels lashed out, he leaped against her rump, pressing his body hard against her. She was trapped as if her hind legs had been hobbled! Through his clothes he could feel her break out in lather. He too was drenched in sweat. Relief and happiness flooded into him as her muscles relaxed. He had won the first skirmish.

He went around now to her head and gently took hold of her halter. "You, so soft-eyed," he said. "You could not hurt me. Not ever. I am not afraid. Why are you afraid? Come," he coaxed, trying the new name softly. "Come, Gau-den-zia." And he led her out into the morning.

Doctor Celli could not hide his surprise. "Colombo!" he shouted to his farmer, who was throwing a pan of soaked acorns to the sow. "Look here! Already she knows who is master."

The farmer and Doctor Celli stood back in amazement while Giorgio lifted her hurt foot and held it between his knees. Carefully he pressed his hand from her hock down her cannon bone and along the tendon to a point just above the fetlock. To his great relief he could tell that the tendon was not bowed.

"The leg," Giorgio said, "should be rested if . . ."

Doctor Celli nodded. "So I told you! A month, maybe."

"No! No!" the boy spoke quickly. "If the tendon bowed out, then she would need rest. But now we got to keep her leg moving. The gristle otherwise will harden."

The men exchanged glances, eyeing each other with doubtful, questioning looks.

Giorgio pretended not to notice. He spoke with a bold sureness that surprised even himself. "If you please," he said, "I now make a poultice of flour and alum for the bruised place, and if you don't mind, we leave at once. It is sixty kilometers to Monticello and I must stop often to rest her."

The farmer disappeared to fetch the flour and alum, and Doctor Celli himself produced the bridle.

"She does not willingly take the bit," he said. "I will help you."

Giorgio smiled and shook his head. He led the mare inside her stable and cross-tied her to iron rings fastened to opposite walls. Then he saw that underneath her chin was a raw, red place. He thought a moment, and took from his pocket the rabbit's foot. Much as he prized it for a good luck charm, he skinned it and wrapped the soft fur about the chinstrap of the bridle.

"Now, Gaudenzia," he said as if he were talking to a small child, "with rabbit's fur the strap will not chafe the sore spot."

It took only a little firmness to slip the bit between her teeth and to adjust the throat latch. And she actually pushed her leg against Giorgio's hand while he bound the poultice in place.

For as long as he lived, Giorgio knew he would never forget this day. Of all the masters Gaudenzia had known, she had singled *him* out as the one to trust! Why else did she let him leap aboard without bolting? Why else did she travel the mountainous country with scarce any favoring of her hurt leg? Why else did she swivel her ears to pull in his talk, or a snatch of his song?

The trip took all day, with Giorgio walking up the hills and riding down. Whenever they came to a stream, he let her wade into it, let her paw and plash to her heart's content. It was a remedy Babbo had handed down. "One thing you must know about horses," he had said time and again. "Soak hurt feet and legs in mountain streams, and you leave behind the fever and the pain."

Giorgio wished he could make the day last forever. In riding, he and Gaudenzia fitted together as if some sculptor had molded them all of one piece. In walking, they were a team, enjoying the cool wind in their faces and the warm sun on their backs.

It was good to see the country again! The little checkerboard farms with rows of grapevines holding hands, and hills swelling away to the horizon, and cypress trees marching bold and black against the sky.

They met farmers with guns on their shoulders, and lean dogs nosing for game. And they saw oxen slow-footing as they turned over the clods of earth.

They saw strawstacks, layered golden and brown, like mocha tortes. At thought of the tortes Giorgio was suddenly hungry. Standing at the side of the road, one arm through the reins, he ate his bread and salami and watched Gaudenzia graze. He wondered how far into the distance she could see. He studied her purple-brown eyes, but all he saw in them was his own reflection.

The sun was slipping into the folds of the mountains when they reached the wild loveliness of the Maremma. Never had it seemed so boundless. To Giorgio it was not lonely looking at all. He bristled at the thought. To him the tangle of brush and brake was beautiful, and the wild birds more plentiful than anywhere, and the autumn weeds winking bright and yellow in the roughed-up land. He stopped at a small wayside shrine decorated with a bouquet of dahlias, and asked a blessing for his new responsibility.

As they took off again, he noticed that the mare had lifted one of the flowers from the shrine. He laughed to the wind and the echo rolled back to him.

At last, in the thickening twilight, they wound up the hill to the huddled houses of Monticello. He clucked to Gaudenzia, asking her to trot the last few meters home in triumph. Her hoofbeats alerted the whole village.

Shutters flew open. Heads popped out. Voices shouted.

"Look! Look what Giorgio brings home! A white scarecrow!" And the children made a sing-song of it. "A white scarecrow! A white scarecrow!"

"Hey, Giorgio! She's got ribs like a washboard!"

"If you sell her for nothing, I wouldn't buy."

The jokes were all good natured, and in high spirits Giorgio leaped from Gaudenzia's back and led her to Pippa's stable. But Pippa was not there. In her place stood a red motor scooter with Babbo's old cap on the handlebars.

For a moment Giorgio felt grief. Then he wiped it away as if it were a cobweb. He had to think ahead now. "It is better Pippa is not here," he said to the mare. "Nobody now can be jealous." He showed Gaudenzia around, showed her the old donkey cart and the trunk with the oats in it and the big wide windows. "You have only a little alley for view," he explained, "but nicer than Doctor Celli's stable with windows too high for seeing out. No?"

As he took off her bridle, she rubbed her head against him where the leathers had been. He sighed happily, feeling singled out and special again. "At last you have come to me!" he said. Then he went to the trunk and scooped up a measure of grain. Before pouring it into the manger he sifted it between his fingers, removing the dried grasshoppers and beetles.

It was late evening when his family returned home from the farm where they had been gathering grapes. But they all had to see the mare, and admire her points, even though she was not in a welcoming mood.

That night when Giorgio went to bed in the family bedroom he did not mind that Emilio, with arms and legs flung wide, slept crosswise, taking up most of the bed. As the wind blew cool, he pulled up the cover, making it snug about Emilio's back. It was good to feel cozy and warm and welcome; good to belong to a family again.

Before he dozed off, he saw through the open window a fingernail moon far away above the mountain. A new moon, a new mare, a new beginning . . .

*Chapter XIX*

NO MORNING GLORY

When Giorgio awoke the next morning he felt whole and strong and full of purpose. He hurried at once to the barn and set to work. He grained Gaudenzia and gave her fresh water. Then he nailed hardwood boards over the lower half of the two windows. "In case of kicking," he explained to an early visitor, "splinters of wood are better than splinters of glass."

Word quickly flew from house to house that "the little runt of Monticello" was back home with a race mare. Neighbors, relatives, friends came from far and near just to look. A few recognized that she was Farfalla, the cart horse, but they seemed puzzled by her fineness, awed by the Arabian head. In her shabby harness they had never really noticed her before. They were not speechless, however. The advice Giorgio got was enough to fill a book.

"Worm her! It is the worms that make her thin."

"Mix tiny pinches of snuff with her grain."

"Pull her shoes at once, before she kicks you over the moon."

Giorgio listened with only half his mind. He wondered how he was going to handle the curious visitors and get his work done, too. But the novelty soon wore off. For everyone, that is, except Giorgio.

Each time he opened the door to her stable he felt the same inward excitement as on the first day he had seen her. And each time he held the water bucket for her to drink, or felt her head scratching against his shoulder, the joy was so deep the whole world seemed different. It wasn't exactly a fatherly feeling he had; it was stronger, more fantastic, as though he lived in ancient times and some oracle had said: "Fate has given her to you. You, Giorgio Terni, are all to her—master, teacher, god. Now prepare her for the great battle of the Palio."

Never before had Giorgio paid much attention to calendars; he had enjoyed the pictures on them and noticed the holidays. But now, suddenly, the pages of the months flashed and signaled importantly.

Hanging on a nail in Gaudenzia's barn, beside the bunches of drying anise-seed, were several dusty old calendars. The top two were 1948 and 1949, but they would do. He tore off the first eight months of 1948 and wrote on the bottom of the page marked *Settembre*, "Rest her."

On *Ottobre* he wrote, "Walk her four kilometers."

On *Novembre*, "Walk three, jog one."

On *Dicembre*, "Walk two, jog two."

On the 1949 calendar, for *Gennaio* he wrote, "Walk one, jog three, gallop one."

On *Febbraio*, "Two-two-two."

On *Marzo*, "Walk one, trot two, gallop three."

Then he put ditto marks on *Aprile* and *Maggio*, and for *Giugno* wrote, "Walk one, jog three, gallop three and one-half."

As he lifted the page for *Luglio* he solemnly circled the second, the Festival of the Visitation of the Madonna, the day of the Palio. He turned then to face Gaudenzia and found her blinking at him, yawning in contentment.

"Our life-threads squinch closer and closer together. No?" he asked of her. He wanted to say more, to show her he grasped the total wonder of their fate, but there were things he could not put into words.

With the training program laid out on paper, Giorgio went to work with a frenzy. He felt that no force on earth could stop him. Each day he glanced at the calendar on the wall as if it were a generalissimo barking out orders.

One morning when Gaudenzia stood bridled and ready for exercise, Babbo burst into the stable with startling news.

"The government!" he announced proudly. "It has jobs—for you and for me!"

"Jobs?"

"Si, si. Down the slope of Mount Amiata we must plant trees."

"But already there are many!"

"More they need, to hold the soil. You see," he explained, "the rain washes away the earth, causing great damages. The pay is not much," he added, "but it helps. We both go."

Giorgio's stomach rose and fell. I will have to tell Babbo "no," he thought. On the calendar I have already fixed the plans for Gaudenzia. She is in training for battle; we cannot stop now.

"Babbo," he said, "every morning I take Gaudenzia to the road that winds round the hills. We walk, and we jog, and then we begin the gallops and . . ." He broke off as a sudden thought struck him. Instead of working Gaudenzia in the morning, he would plant the trees, and take her out at night. Was not the Palio held at sundown? Why not accustom her to the late hour?

He smiled. "But from now on I train her by night. Yes, Babbo, I will go with you. We will plant the trees together."

Later that day the father proudly told the townfolk, "That Giorgio of mine, he makes of Gaudenzia no morning glory! Horses has time clocks in their heads. The morning bloomers wilt by noon. Oh, that boy, he thinks like the four-footed!"

As the days grew shorter, the workouts grew longer, more intense. Long walks with little jogs gave way to long jogs with little walks. By starlight, by moonlight, the white mare rounded the curves of Mount Amiata like some floating phantom of the night. She was never extended, never pushed. Without anyone's telling him how or why, Giorgio knew he had to build up her confidence in herself. Always he stopped short of what she could do. There was plenty of time to reach the peak. The real mountain, he knew, was not Amiata.

October, November, and December were torn off the calendar. In January there were many days of mist and drizzle when Giorgio still had to work, planting trees. Then no one passed the stable for hours at a time, and Gaudenzia's nervous twitching came on again and she took to crib-biting. One dismal evening when he came to bridle her, she stood grunting as she clamped her teeth on her manger, sucking air into her stomach. Giorgio tried fastening his belt around her neck, loose enough so that she could munch grain, but tight enough to prevent her opening her jaws for swallowing air. It worked! After this, on rainy days, he made her wear the belt, and all went well. And so, regardless of weather, they left the stable each evening at the same hour, clattering down the stony lanes of Monticello, and out upon the lonely road cleft in the hill.

Nothing was too good for Gaudenzia. He gave her rubdowns, first with straw, then with burlap bags. He borrowed the flour sifter from home, and each measure of grain he sifted free of bugs and dust, saving the dead beetles for the kittens. He begged old sheeting from his mother and spent precious lire buying cotton and alcohol with which to bandage her forelegs. "You cannot even imagine," he told Gaudenzia, "how firm we make your legs." Sometimes she threatened to bite him as he worked, but she never did. More often she lipped the back of his sweater, in the way a dam gently nibbles along the neck of her colt.

Giorgio lived all day—digging and planting—for the night. He might have been sticking faggots in the earth for all he knew. His mind was everywhere else: on the calendar in the stable, taking the curves of the mountain, putting on his helmet for the race. Trumpets and drums beat like blood in his ears. Unconsciously he began whistling the "March of the Palio." It made Babbo and all the other men work better, happier.

The months of winter passed, not in days and weeks, but in developing Gaudenzia's wind and stamina. When Giorgio came home each night, mud-spattered and hungry, his mother reheated the soup and stood by as he drank it. One night when his hair was wet with snow, and his jacket sagging and sopping, she cried, "Giorgio, Giorgio, Giorgio, why can't you let up?"

The boy stopped eating. "Mamma, I can't!" he said

firmly. "Have you forgot the Palio? Three times around Il Campo is four and a half kilometers. She must go the whole way and still be strong at the finish!"

By March she was galloping three kilometers.

On the fifteenth of May, Giorgio walked her to nearby Casole d'Elsa and entered her in a race on a straightaway course. She flew ahead at the start, and with no sign of difficulty, led all the way. It was a stunning triumph for the mare and her young trainer.

The whole family took a long time deciding where to hang the little red-and-white flag she won. Teria chose the spot. "Here," she said, "beside the cupboard. On this wall the sun comes just before setting."

Often, when no one was looking, Giorgio ran his fingertips over the painting of the white mare on the red silk. Was this the work of a soothsayer? He read the artist's name in the turf beneath her flying hoofs. How did the man know that a white mare would win, and so picture her instead of a black, or a bay? And under the date of the race was painted a golden crown bright with jewels. Had the oracle spoken to the artist, too? Or had he seen a boy flying in the night on a white phantom?

Once when Babbo caught Giorgio fingering the little humps of oil paint that made the jewels of the crown, he pulled the boy aside. "Jesters," he said, not wanting him to be hurt, "sometimes wear the crown like king and queen. Maybe that artist fellow, he dangles the carrot before Gaudenzia only to tease."

*Chapter XX*

A SIMPLE PLAN

June! The hallway into summer. The season for strong happenings, the season for living. Giorgio's mind was on tip-toe. Looking at his calendar one morning he thought, in a flash, of the ski slide on Mount Amiata, saw the skiers toiling up and up for one breathless whoosh into space. Now he knew how they felt. For months he and Gaudenzia had been toiling up and up for the wild two minutes of glory that was the Palio.

The days of June neither dragged nor flew. They were as alike as echoes. Walk Gaudenzia one kilometer, jog her three, gallop her three and a half. Bandage her hind legs, bandage her forelegs. Grain her, a handful more each day. Cut down her hay. And always, the inner command pounding through him: Don't let her reach the peak until July. Climb, climb, climb. Bring her right up *to* it.

In the last week of June, the long-awaited message from the Chief-of-the-Guards reached Giorgio. "Come to Siena! At once!" was all it said.

By cockcrow on the morning after, boy and mare were on their way, trotting along gay-spirited, as if the wheatfields spattered with wild red poppies, and the hills high-rising to the sky, and all the creatures in it were theirs. Gaudenzia wanted to race every moving thing—a rabbit skirting the edge of the road, a hound streaking for a bird—the bird, too. Her friskiness, her eagerness to go filled him with a pride so strong he had to whistle to let the steam of his happiness escape. Nine months ago, with a bandage on her heel, she had slow-footed her way over this same road. Now, like Mercury with wings, she was returning.

A solitary shepherd, hungry for human company, ran out on the road and invited Giorgio to share the meal he was preparing over an open fire. He pointed his crook at Gaudenzia.

"*Magnifico!*" he exclaimed, with a smile so wide it showed the dark hole where two of his teeth were missing.

"Magnifica!" Giorgio laughingly corrected him. "She is a mare!" He joined the herdsman in a meal of goat cheese and grilled eel. And while the mare grazed, her eyes ranging with the cloud of sheep, the lonely herder questioned Giorgio about his plans. Then he poured out his own heart. He too had a dream. He would teach a young boy to herd, teach him just where to noon the sheep, and which ones to watch in a storm. Then he would be free for a little while, and he would walk to Siena, and there, before he died, he would witness with his own eyes the manifestation of the Palio!

It was all Giorgio could do to break away from the man and his dream. With their final handshake the herder for the first time became mute. Wistfully, he watched Giorgio mount Gaudenzia and rein her out onto the road. When at last he found his voice, he cupped his hands and called out after them: "Magnifica!"

In Siena, too, the mare created admiration, but it was thinned with doubts and forebodings. Entering the city through the Arch of Porta Romana in the early evening, Giorgio could feel at once the general air of agitation. The usual flow of promenaders had given way to excited knots of men choking the traffic. Bruco! Oca! Onda! Tartuca! The names of the contradas punctuated the talk. And town eyes were staring his way.

"What a beautiful beast goes there!" a voice said. And the same voice asked, "Boy, where did you get her? What are you going to do with her?"

Giorgio turned and saw a grizzle-headed old man, the center of a group. "It's a long story, Signore," he answered. "She used to be Farfalla, but now she—"

The man did not let him finish. "Eh?" he exclaimed. "Can this be Farfalla returned from the dead?"

And another said, "A fine parade horse she would make. But for the race?" The shoulders owning the voice shrugged.

And then Giorgio overheard, "Would you wish to draw her for *your* contrada?"

A whole chorus answered, "No! No!" It was as if her tortured limping in last year's Palio was a memory too fresh to be wiped out.

Giorgio himself flinched at the recollection. He touched his heels to Gaudenzia and hurried her through the crowd. "How they feel about you, I do not care," he told himself. "It is better so. Popular horses are nearly killed by too many sweets, too much petting and pulling of tail-hairs for souvenir. I believe, and the Chief believes!"

He found the Chief striding across Il Campo, heading for his home. They saw each other at the same moment.

"Giorgio!" the big man shouted, and his arms flung wide apart, as though he would clasp the boy and the mare both. "How are you? How is it with our *cavallina?* Tell me all about her! Don't keep me one minute more in this anxious waiting."

Giorgio suddenly felt shy. He answered with two little words. "All fine."

"That I can see!" the Chief laughed. "The mare, she is rekindled!" He stepped now in front of Gaudenzia, pulled off his white gloves, and with both hands felt of her chest and forearms. "Not even sweating," he nodded in approval. "Come, let us walk to the stable, and while walking you will tell me how she goes in her work.

Then, after she is bedded down, you will come to my home where we can engage in serious talk."

The stable was midway of a narrow downhill alley with walls high-rising on either side. Giorgio's spirits plummeted at its darkness. It did have a window, but it was covered by a curtain of gunny sacking. There were two stalls divided by heavy planking. The one nearer the door was occupied by a bay gelding, and the other, deeply strawed, awaited Gaudenzia.

"To find stable room is very difficult," the Chief was explaining. "But Morello here is a good horse and the two will become friends and help each other to forget the Maremma. He, too, comes from your wilderness."

Across the partition Gaudenzia and Morello began at once to get acquainted—first in screams, then nips, and at last in low whinnies.

"How quick they make friends!" the Chief grinned. "Now then, the hay is piled here, the grain is in the sack yonder, and the medicines in the cabinet. Now you can take over."

Giorgio noted the racks already filled, the water buckets brimming. He would come back later to grain and groom Gaudenzia and to remove the gunny-sack curtain.

He followed the Chief to his home, which perched on a ledge of rock like an eagle's nest. The view was miniature compared to the world of the Maremma. Below was a tiny dim valley, and climbing the opposite hillside were busy little farm plots. But the same deep sky was overhead and the same stars beginning to punch holes in the blue.

The Chief's wife and daughter greeted Giorgio with politeness and relief. "The supper is ready," the Signora said with a hot-stove smile. "I would not want the chicken to cook a moment longer."

The meal was a feast such as Giorgio had not tasted since his days at the Ramallis'. First there was a piping hot broth of chicken with tiny pearls of dough swimming along the bottom. Then came a beautiful plate of antipasto—black olives, and mushrooms in oil, and little white onions, and small green peppers, and anchovies curved into tight nests, with a caper on each. Giorgio was encouraged to take something of everything. And still he had room for a drumstick and breast of chicken, and a baked tomato stuffed with ground beef.

All of this he sluiced down with a red Chianti wine which he thriftily diluted with water as though he were at home.

The Chief helped himself to the food sparingly, and in silence. He seemed preoccupied, brooding. But Giorgio ate heartily. The Signora beamed at him. "For a small man, as you are," she said, appreciatively, "you have *un bel appetito.*"

Giorgio felt his face flush and his ears redden at the half-and-half compliment.

With the dessert of fruit and cheeses on the table,

the wife and daughter disappeared into the kitchen. The silence grew heavy. The Chief pushed back his plate without touching the food. At last the moment for talk had arrived.

But the words did not come. He ran his finger around the inside of his collar and cleared his throat. He got up and stood at the open door, looking out upon the night. He came back and sat down again. Then, gripping the edge of the table, he blurted out, "My boy, the Palio is not going to be as we dreamed it."

Giorgio swallowed whole the apricot in his mouth. It was as though an icy hand had gripped his throat.

"You see, the *people* want beautiful horses such as Gaudenzia, but the judges, no!"

Giorgio's voice sank back so deep inside him it was scarcely audible. "But why?"

The Chief took a breath. For the boy's sake he wanted to sound matter-of-fact, to ease him gently into disappointment. "The news of Gaudenzia's win at Casole d'Elsa has spread to Siena. All at once she is known as the get of Sans Souci, a full blood Arab. And the full-bloods are not wanted."

"But, Signore, she is only half-bred. Her dam was a farm horse."

"I know, I know," the Chief answered in irritation. "But because she is now too beautiful, too well-trained, the rejection may come."

Giorgio waited in numbness.

"High-mettled Arabians have caprices, the judges say. Besides, the turns of the course are too perilous and the layer of earth over the cobblestones too thin for a full-blood with the delicate toothpick legs."

There was a momentary pause as the Chief's daughter brought in two small cups of coffee.

"You see, Giorgio, we Sienese are like moles burrowing, always digging into our past. I have heard the judges say, as if only yesterday it happened, how in the year 1500 Cesare Borgio's big stallion reared on his hind legs and in coming back to earth hit the starting rope so hard he could not run in the Palio. And in 1885, the purebred La Gorgona cracked up in the last Prova, her legs brittle like eggshell. And you, Giorgio, you must remember Habana? You remember when she flew into the fence, and broke the boards to splinters!"

"But Signore! It happens with the mixed blood, too. Have they forgot Turbolento?"

"*He* fell, Giorgio. But the others? One might say they destroyed themselves."

Anger lit Giorgio's eyes. "Signore! This you should have told me before! Why did you send for Gaudenzia and me? Why did you let me nourish all the hopes to win?"

The Chief wiped his face tiredly. "I do not know, truly. Perhaps the hope is in me, too. Perhaps the hope is stronger than the reality. I fear, Giorgio," he said again, "the Palio is not going to be as we dreamed it."

"Signore! Shake yourself!" Giorgio's anger turned to wild appeal. His words tumbled out bravely, recklessly. "Something we can do! Something we *must* do! Think!" He took hold of the man's sleeve, actually shaking him in his eagerness.

The Chief closed his eyes thoughtfully. "What comes to mind," he said at last, "is a very simple plan. Maybe too simple."

"Tell me! Tell me!"

Something of the old vigor crept into the Chief's voice. "Listen well, my boy. In the trials when the horses are selected, you must make Gaudenzia appear mature, sensible; an average beast."

Giorgio nodded, listening with every fiber.

"And in her workouts she must appear tranquil."

"That is easy! Easy! What else?"

"Wherever you make talk, you must say how her dam was a poor old farm horse and how she herself was a cart horse for many years, and her colts were nothing at all, good only for the slaughterhouse."

"I will!"

"Margherita," the Chief called to his daughter, "our coffees are now cold." He turned back to Giorgio. "Only one thing is in our favor. You see . . ."

There was a pause as the coffees came and he liberally spooned sugar into both cups. "Because all the contradas think her nervous, unpredictable, none will ask for agreement from you to help another horse to win."

Giorgio sighed in deep relief. "Of that I am glad. When I am on Gaudenzia I am *simpatico* only to her. But why is it no one has ever come to me to make the secret agreement?"

The Chief could not help chuckling. "'The runt of Monticello', they say, 'is young and green like new spear of wheat. We do not make agreements with a boy so little he has to have double lining in his helmet to keep it on.'"

The man suddenly went silent. What if Giorgio were not asked to ride Gaudenzia in the Palio? He held his tongue. The boy had had enough worries for one night.

*Chapter XXI*

HALF-BRED

Tuesday, June 29. Morning. The whole city seething in warlike impatience. Il Campo in battle array. Everything ready for the trial of the horses. The stout railing around the shell to keep the people from spilling onto curves. The tiers of seats rising in front of the palaces and cobblestones. The mattresses, upright, lining the treacherous curves. The tiers of seats rising in front of the palaces and shops. The high platforms for the judges and dignitaries. The bomb cage on stilts, looking like an oversized parrot cage, ready for the charge of gunpowder.

And people converging from all directions, talking excitedly with their hands, their voices. Which horses will be chosen to run? Surely not the old one who has twelve years! Surely not the little one with the ewe neck? Surely not Gaudenzia with the hot blood in her veins?

The lone hand on the clock of the Mangia Tower points to nine. Within the courtyard of the Palazzo Pubblico seventeen horses and riders are ready. Giorgio is ready. He has done everything the Chief asked. And more. He has plastered sculptor's clay on Gaudenzia's legs to make them look coarse, like those of any cold-blooded hack. But there is nothing he can do to coarsen her fine, intelligent head.

Out in the shell, a little insect of a man, known as the Spider, climbs his ladder, touches a match to the gunpowder in the cage, and with a thundering *bang* the trials have begun! Four horses prance out of the palace courtyard. At the starter's signal they take off, leaping over the rope before it touches the earth. At the very first curve one horse falls, skids across the track like a slab of ice. The crowd screams as the horse scrambles to his feet. He will be rejected. It is Fate.

Another group is called. No falls this time, but the horses are not evenly matched. They straggle along like knots on a string.

And still another group, while Gaudenzia waits. She listens to the hoofbeats. Flecks of foam come out on her body. Her whole being asks: Why are we not out there with the others? She whinnies out after them. Giorgio lays quieting hands on her, soothes them along her neck and withers. He is glad her mantle is gray so the sudsy foam does not show.

At last she is called with the remaining five. Her long-reaching legs are ready. Her heart and lungs are ready. Giorgio mounts. His heart tightens in sudden doubt. Is speed her only virtue? Has she learned obedience? He wets his parched lips, prays fiercely. "O Holy One, let her be in the middle! Don't let her run away and set the pace. Let her just be middling!"

The starter steps on the lever. The rope, set free, snakes crazily to earth. Five horses leap over it. They're away! Evenly! Past the scaffold of the judges, past the Fonte Gaia. One horse tries to wing out at the incoming street of San Pietro, but the others are moving in a bunch. "Oh, Mamma mia! Don't let her win! Don't let her!"

She is third at the curve of San Martino, and third at the Casato. Suddenly she asks to arrow out in front, but she feels the bit pulling up into her mouth, exerting more and more pressure on her tongue. She slows. She lets Giorgio hold her. She obeys!

Out of the first realization, like the first glint of sunlight from behind a cloud, Giorgio feels an unutterable joy. Twice around, and three times around, she lets him hold her! In third place she finishes, all her fire inheld. The trials are over!

While the judges pondered and debated their decisions, Giorgio rode into the cool courtyard of the Palazzo. Here were only the sweating horses and the men, all of them bound together in the misery of waiting.

The Chief-of-the-Guards, immaculate in his starched white uniform, looked in and strode over to Giorgio. There was a smile of incredulity on his face.

"I salute you!" he said. "Gaudenzia's disguise was *bellissima*! When first I saw her at the starting rope, it seemed I dreamt with open eyes. Even a sculptor, I think, could not have done a better work on living skin."

He made no effort to hide his happiness, for already he knew the results of the trials. Already a deputy was fastening a disc numbered 10 to Gaudenzia's cheek strap to show that she had been chosen.

The Chief led Giorgio and the mare out into the Piazza, into a corral where the ten horses would be on display as at an auction. The big difference was that here a horse could not be bought; not for any price. It was assigned to a contrada as irrevocably as a child is born to certain parents. Here all was luck. A miniscule slip of paper in a tiny capsule would tell which contrada would win the best horse.

Suspense was growing intolerable. There was wild shouting for the favorites. Voices came piercing and crashing around Giorgio.

"We want Ravu!"

"We want Uganda!"

"We want Rosetta!"

An official groom shoved Giorgio to one side, took hold of Gaudenzia. There was now no need for Giorgio. And then, in a flash, he realized there was no need for him anywhere! The awfulness struck him. For nine months he had been blindly running up a dead-end street. Feeling sick and bereft, he went back into the empty courtyard. He picked up Gaudenzia's rub rag, hung it on a peg. He made meaningless motions of tidying up. But even here, away from the crowd, he saw the whole scene in his mind—the Mayor and the captains at the long table, the urns containing the capsules, the pages and trumpeters waiting. And then, as in a storm, when thunder rumbles and ricochets from rock to rock, the voices came booming against the Palazzo wall and into the very courtyard:

"Number seven, Ravu, to the Ram!"

He could hear the Rams roaring with joy for the favorite.

"Number nine, Pinocchio, to the Giraffe!"

Men and boys howled in derision, "Long Neck gets Long Nose! Long Neck gets Long Nose."

The roaring was uncontrolled; it subsided only while the capsules were being opened.

"Number one to the Wolf!"

"Number five to the Dragon!"

"Number two to the Tower!"

"Number ten to Onda, the Wave!"

Giorgio shot out of the courtyard, but the way to the corral was blocked. By the time he could wriggle through, the drawing was over! And, suddenly, there was trumpet music, and drums beating wild, and the barbaresco of the Onda was leading Gaudenzia to their stable. In an agony of emptiness Giorgio melted into the throng, went tagging along like some outsider. With no halter or bridle to hold, his hands felt awkward, useless. A piece of his heart was going away with Gaudenzia.

Should he catch up with the barbaresco and tell him about the crib-biting? Should he offer his belt? Should he offer to clean Gaudenzia's stable tomorrow, and tomorrow?

No, everything was out of his control now. In the next moments he lived a lifetime. No contrada had asked him to be their fantino. Why should they? In two Palios he had not won.

A fight started in the crowd. A young boy from the Dragon and one from the Tower began with friendly roughness, yanking each other's caps, then grabbing contrada scarves, then arms swinging, and fists pummeling. Giorgio wanted to join in, to throw one and then the other flat on the ground. Anything would be better than having nothing to do. Someone in the crowd recognized Giorgio, pointed a finger at him. "Hey, fantino! Afoot now? Ha! Ha!"

Giorgio leaped at the lanky fellow, ready to land a left jab, when suddenly his arm was wrenched behind him. A strange, deep voice commanded: "Hold there, Giorgio! Let up! Street fighting is for boys. *You* face the real battle, the battle of the Palio."

Giorgio looked into the eyes of a gentleman. At once he recognized the man. He had just seen him on the platform with all the officials. "You!" he gulped for air. "You are General Barbarulli, leader of the Onda!"

The General smiled. Then he linked his arm into Giorgio's, and above the din spoke into his ear: "The Chief-of-the-Town-Guards tells me it is you who trained Gaudenzia."

Giorgio nodded, scarcely breathing.

"A stroke of chance has given her to the Onda, but," the General slowed his words, emphasizing each one, "but with Giorgio Terni as her fantino, that is not luck. *That* is destiny."

## Chapter XXII

### SPEAK! SPEAK!

Immediately after Giorgio's talk with General Barbarulli, four bodyguards were assigned to him. They were tall, strapping fellows—Carlo, Pinotto, Enzio, and Nello. Their eyes followed him wherever he went. They never let him alone. Even at night he could feel them peering at him, boring right through him in the dark.

"Am I a dog on a leash?" he asked, trying to make a joke of it.

The young men only laughed at the trapped-animal look of him. "We attach ourselves to you," Carlo said kindly, "to prevent rival contradas from coming with secret offers."

"But no one will! Even the Chief-of-the-Guards tells me that. He says I have not yet seen enough Palios."

The boys agreed. "But we must also protect you from street fights," Enzio explained. "We must save your hands. They are small as . . ."

"I know." Giorgio bit his lips, then supplied the missing words. "Small as girl's hands!"

It was scarcely any relief to swing up on Gaudenzia and ride twice a day in the Provas. For even then he was not free. He knew that he was being carefully observed, his every action noticed and weighed.

Why, he asked himself, did it take two Palios to teach him all the rules and regulations leading up to the big race? He answered himself honestly. Turbolento and Lirio, the horses he had ridden last year, had been little more than names to him—no, they had almost been nameless. But Gaudenzia was a part of his very life.

So now, for the first time, he was terrified by a rule that had not really concerned him before. According to a proclamation of the Grand Duke in 1719, the choice of the fantinos is not made final and official until the day of the Palio. If through Giorgio's carelessness Gaudenzia were kicked and lamed as in last year's Prova, he could be dismissed abruptly. He had been hired, yes, but he could still be replaced, even on the very morning of the Palio!

Thus, tortured by uncertainty, he took great care to

keep Gaudenzia clear of the other horses, and to bring her in slowly at the finish of each Prova.

At night, however, he and Gaudenzia knew no restraints. When the moon rode high, he took secret delight in waking his bodyguards, who slept on mattresses in his room.

"Wake up, or I go alone!" he told the sleepy young giants.

Grumbling, they dressed and went out with him into the night. They pounded heavily on the locked door of the stable of Onda. It was easier to wake Gaudenzia than the sleeping barbaresco.

"Open!" shouted Giorgio, and it was the mare's stomping and pawing that finally woke the groom. She remembered well the routine of galloping in the dark, and the time clock in her mind said, "Now."

The city lay asleep. In the twisty streets, small yellow flames flickered here and there before shrines to the Virgin Mary. But in the shell of Il Campo the moon shone clear and bold.

*This* was the real Prova! The four young men and the barbaresco, watching in the deep moon shadow, nearly forgot themselves in awed excitement. They were fully awake now. They wanted to shout and cheer at the smooth-flying gallop. Around the treacherous curves Gaudenzia went flying as if she were suspended on pulleys. Only an occasional spark from her hoofs showed she was earthbound.

In less than an hour they were all back in bed again.
For Giorgio and Gaudenzia, sleep was sweet after the
moonlight gallop.

July first, the day before the Palio, turned hot, with a
brassy sun. The morning Prova took place at the hour
of nine. General Barbarulli was on hand to observe, and
afterward he stopped Giorgio on the way to the stable.
He looked at Gaudenzia, but not at her head. He seemed
to see only the heel that had been hurt last year.

"She goes sound?" He clipped out the questions. "She goes true? Her legs, are they cool after the running?"

"Si, si, General."

"The Provas are nearly over, son. Already there have been four. If all goes well in the last two, you will be fantino for the Contrada of the Wave, and tomorrow your name will be inscribed in the archives, officially."

Giorgio managed an anxious nod. He waited for the General's next words.

"Thus far she has not won a single Prova." Something in the man's voice told Giorgio that he was in no way displeased.

"Tonight," he went on, "is the banquet before the Palio. As you know, it is the great meeting of our people. You must come and you will be seated between Captain Tortorelli and myself. Your bodyguards will bring you at the hour of eight. From you only a short speech will be expected."

"A speech! Me? A speech!" Giorgio grabbed a handful of Gaudenzia's mane as if he might topple off. The bodyguards came up then to accompany him to the stable. His lips moved drily. "A speech I must make," he mumbled in deep misery.

All that afternoon Giorgio struggled with pencil and paper. As the result of his labors he produced only three small sentences. These he copied neatly on a clean sheet and folded it into the breast pocket of his good suit.

Promptly at the stated hour Pinotto, Carlo, Enzio, and Nello led him toward the church of the Wave. He felt like a prisoner on his way to execution, as they wound in single file through the narrow streets, through the arch of San Guiseppe, then through the doors of the church itself, and down the wide, winding staircase into another world deep under the sanctuary.

Giorgio stood gaping at the splendor. The banquet hall was high-vaulted and vast. Already many people were seated in their places at the rows of tables, but some were still standing in clusters, deep in conversation. With the entrance of the burly guards towering over the slight figure of Giorgio, all faces turned in his direction.

"Look! Our fantino! He comes!"

General Barbarulli signaled the bodyguards to come to the speakers' platform. For one frozen moment Giorgio saw the scene and remembered. Yes! There was the long table on the raised flooring, and the snow-pure cloth spread over it, and the serious-faced men seated on one side only. It was like the painting of the Last Supper, the one hanging above his mother's and father's bed. Overawed, he wanted to bolt, wanted to hide behind his bodyguards, but they were gone! They had stepped down from the platform and melted into the crowd.

The General and Captain Tortorelli welcomed Giorgio with cordial handshakes. Nervously, he felt for his speech in the place where his pocket should be, but his hand felt cotton, not wool, and he looked down and saw he had no pocket! He remembered now he was wearing the uniform of the Wave, the white-and-blue fantino uniform which the contrada had sent over. His speech was still in his room, in the pocket of his good suit hanging on the peg!

The Captain shook his hand a second time. "Do not worry," he said encouragingly. "All good fantinos are nervous. Those who joke have a gross heart." Then he introduced Giorgio to the vicar, the chancellor, the captain's assistant, the steward, and all the councilors.

When the food was served, Giorgio ate, though he hardly knew what he ate. His ears heard the stirring battle songs of defiance, of threats, but all the while his mind was trying to recall those three little sentences he had painstakingly written down. They were gone from him. Gone as completely as if some other hand had formed them.

"We are all united in the warm atmosphere of this dinner. In joy and friendship . . ."

"Oh, Mamma mia!" breathed Giorgio, dropping his fork with a clatter. "The speeches, they begin!"

"We of the Wave," the General was intoning, "regard this, our banquet hall, as our other home, our other hearth-place of Love and Brotherhood. Many of our families have separated for the Palio, each member having gone back to the contrada where he was born. In their place, many of us are hosts to some kinsman or friend. So first we greet and welcome those who are our guests."

Of one accord the *contradaioli* applauded.

The General smiled affably. "The Palio lifts us out of the everyday life," he continued. "We are caught up in the golden net of hope, of ambition, of glory. In four hundred years the magnificent colors of the Wave—blue for the billows and white for the foam—have won thirty-nine victories! Will Gaudenzia and Giorgio make it forty?"

"Si! Si! Si!" Wild cries bounced from wall to wall.

Giorgio listened in an agony of suspense. He could feel his chest going in and out against the place where his pocket and his speech should have been. "Please, O Mother of Perpetual Help, let him talk on and on! Let him forget I am here. Or maybe you could make an earthquake . . . or an eruption like Vesuvius . . ."

But the only eruption was a burst of applause as the

General sat down and Captain Tortorelli arose.

Giorgio closed his eyes.

Captain Tortorelli half-closed his eyes, too, but *he* was in ecstasy. "How beautiful is the Piazza of Siena with ten fantinos in battle!" His voice resounded through the great hall. "Some call them ten assassins. Yes, the eyes of an assassin are dangerous, but in the danger they are fiercely beautiful."

Giorgio began to shake all over. The Captain was making a half turn toward him, was facing him now, speaking to him, and the force of his breath caused the hairs on Giorgio's head to quiver. "*Fate* is Queen of the Palio!" the voice rolled on. "We can prepare for victory, morally and materially, but never certainly. Only Fate and the fantino can decide between victory and defeat.

"Some tasks," he concluded, "need a big man. Others, a small one. Some fantinos are big and strong, but some are bird-light and think more of their mount than of their own safety. Giorgio Terni, you are such a one." He raised his glass in a toast to the boy at his side. "Our fate is in your hands."

"Bravo! Bravissimo!" the councilmen and contra-daioli cheered. Then all about there was a great gaping silence—full of eyes, full of question marks. What would the boy say? What promises would he make?

"Speak! Speak!" the people shouted in encouragement.

Giorgio rose to his feet. In the dead silence he nodded to the Captain, and then to the audience. He opened his mouth, but no sound came. He glanced imploringly into the sea of faces, but no one could prompt him. His eyes swept the room, took in the marble angels on either side of the stage. Their cornucopias were sending forth pink and red carnations, but not help. And no help came from the painted dolphin on the wall, its mouth dripping red beads of blood as if it had been caught by some fisherman's hook. And as he stood helpless the silence grew deeper, until it was a roaring in his ears. In desperation he looked upward to the vaulted ceiling, and followed the arches that came together in a central point. It was like the chalice of an Easter lily; no, it was more like the inside of an umbrella.

An *umbrella*! Suddenly the face of the Umbrella Man loomed in front of him, and in spite of his terror he felt strength welling up in him. Now he *wanted* to talk.

"Signori of the Wave!" he began in a voice that had an odd kind of dignity in it. "Gaudenzia and I, we were both reared in the Maremma, and we fit well to each other. Tomorrow we go into battle together. Fear does not choke our courage. For us it is not victory *or* defeat. We think only the one thought—"

"*Vic-to-ry! Vic-to-ry! Viva Giorgio!*"

The crowd had finished his speech for him.

*Chapter XXIII*

### THE HOURS BEFORE

Late on the night of the banquet, while Giorgio lay sleeping, the captains of the contradas were meeting in secret. Some were strengthening old alliances, and some were negotiating new ones. If one contrada, for example, had drawn a poor horse, it would swear to help its ally by every strategy of war.

The results of these meetings were of little concern to Giorgio, for no one, he had been told, would exact any promises from him. And so, exhausted from his speech, he had crawled into bed, and before his bodyguards had stopped joking and smoking he was asleep.

But it was not a peaceful sleep; it was shot through with a frightful dream. In writing down the name "Giorgio Terni" in the archives, the clerk broke his pen on the letter G, and the point flew up, stabbing the man in the throat. Immediately, terrifying things happened. The statue of the she-wolf atop the Palazzo came alive, came howling and hurtling down the column and put a horrible end to the clerk. Then she fell upon Giorgio, slashing him with her fangs and claws until he was unfit to race.

To the shock of crashing thunder Giorgio awoke. He jumped up, leaped over the sprawling figures of his guards, and ran to the window. He stood there, shivering, watching the storm rage. He had a strange sense that the fireball lightning was full of shooting stars, and they seemed to be spelling out the word—"O-f-f-i-c-i-a-l!" He stood there a long time, letting the wind and the rain wash away his dream. At last, chilled to the bone, he went back to bed. Sleep was slow in coming, and brief. At six in the morning the church bells startled him into consciousness. The first summons to the Palio!

His bodyguards, yawning and stretching, looked out in surprise at the rain-soaked land.

"How is it?" Giorgio exclaimed. "If I only turn the doorknob to my room or make tiny tiptoe steps, you hear! But crashing thunder? *No!*"

The guards laughed. As they dressed, they watched

Giorgio fumble with the ties on his fantino uniform. "Could our boy be nervous?" they teased. "And him a veteran of two Palios!"

The bells were still playing when, minutes later, they climbed the steps of Siena's great cathedral. In the shadowy interior, with the candles winking and the faint light coming through the stained-glass windows, Giorgio and the other fantinos knelt at the altar. He glanced at Ivan-the-Terrible on his left, who was riding for the Ram, and at Veleno on his right, fantino for the Giraffe. They were like friendly schoolfellows. Could they, by evening, become enemy warriors? Would the three of them now kneeling prayerfully and peacefully side by side soon be striking each other with their nerbos?

Both fantinos were moving their lips. Giorgio wondered if they were praying to be accepted by their contradas, or praying to win. He looked up at the painting above the altar and read the inscription beneath the Virgin's feet. "O Holy Mother, be thou the fount of peace for Siena, and be thou life for Duccio because he has painted you."

It was hard not to pray for yourself. If Duccio, the great painter, could pray thus . . .

"O Holy Mother," Giorgio whispered, "be thou life for Gaudenzia." He did not realize it was the mare he was praying for, and not himself, so closely were they tuned.

• • •

Nine o'clock came. Time for the last Prova, the final rehearsal before the Palio. The day was windless, the sky gray and cloudy, the track still slippery from last night's rain. Giorgio resolved to take no chances. From the start to the finish he held Gaudenzia almost to a parade canter; he must save every tendon and muscle of her legs. She finished in last place.

As he returned to his room, he wondered if he had done the right thing. Had he been over cautious? Would the Onda approve? Or would they think him lily-livered, not knowing how to ride?

Torn by gnawing anxiety he washed and combed while the guards stood by waiting. In unaccustomed soberness they placed over his arm the blue-and-white jacket of Onda, the very one he would wear in today's Palio, and in his hand the steel helmet. Then as a body they marched him to the Palazzo Pubblico, not into the vast courtyard where the horses are gathered before the race, but into the formal and forbidding Hall of the Magistrates. Here they vanished, and Captain Tortorelli arose out of the gloom and indicated a chair for Giorgio beside him. Other fantinos were already there, seated about a long table, jackets over their arms, helmets in hand. And beside each was his captain.

The city officials now entered the solemnity of the room. The Mayor, in gray-suited dignity, sat down at the head of the table, the starter on his right, then the veterinarian and the Deputy of the Festival. A lean-faced clerk with a pen behind his ear took his place on the Mayor's left. He unrolled a great sheet of paper and laid it out before him. The sheet was empty, except for a margin of tiny colored emblems of all the contradas, and beside them, hair-thin lines waiting to be filled in.

With a dry cough the clerk took the pen from behind his ear and held it poised in midair like a hummingbird before it daggers into a flower.

Giorgio's heart quailed. He tried to stop the racing jumble of his thoughts: last year's death of Turbolento, last night's dream. The hoarfrost voice of the scribe cut off his thinking. Slowly the man called the roll. Each fantino stood up as his contrada was called. Carefully he held up his jacket with both hands so the emblem would plainly show, and waited for his captain to confirm him. This done, the clerk recorded the fantino's name in the big registry, writing with long, even strokes and a flourish of his pen at the end.

When it was Giorgio's turn, his foot caught in the rung of his chair, and it seemed an eternity before he could wrench free. To make matters worse, his hands were shaking so violently that when he held up his jacket the dolphin seemed mockingly alive, undulating through the blue waves of the Onda.

It brought a faint titter from the other fantinos before Captain Tortorelli broke in: "I hereby declare . . ." he paused to clear his throat. "I declare," he repeated, *"Giorgio Terni, fantino for the Onda."*

Never to Giorgio had a man's gruff voice or the scratchy squeak of a pen sounded so sweet. When it was all over, he went out into the vastness of the Piazza. The pigeons were putting on an aerial spectacle, spiralling into the deep sky. Giorgio felt his spirits rise with them.

The Chief-of-the-Guards came up alongside. "I can see from your face," he smiled, "that all is now official."

Giorgio nodded.

"So you and your guards come rest at my house," the Chief said. "For you my wife makes her special zucchini omelette. It sits light in your stomach, and so you sit light on my Gaudenzia! You have now until four o'clock to eat and rest and sip the sweet wine of anticipation."

Giorgio had not visited the eagle's-nest-of-a-house for a whole month, not since the night of his arrival with Gaudenzia. Then, there had been a yellow moon-path on the hillside. Now a watery sun was breaking through the clouds, drawing moisture up in a thick curtain of mist. Only a month, he thought, but leading up to it a whole calendar of months from October to June. And before that, years of training for Signor Ramalli; and before that, Bianca, the Blind One; and before that, way in the beginning, a dusty little Umbrella Man sitting crosslegged by the fountain, reciting the deep mystery of the Palio.

"Come inside! Come inside!" the Chief-of-the-Guards laughed. "Stop gawping. Grapevines and olive groves you have seen before. Now we eat."

Giorgio was glad that no one expected him to eat much, or to talk at all. After the meal Pinotto, Carlo, Enzio, and Nello took their siestas in chairs and on the sofa. But Giorgio and the Chief paced—from balcony to dining room to kitchen and back again.

The afternoon wore slowly on. From the distance came the murmur of Tuscans and tourists pouring through the city's gates. The swelling noise rolled into the house through doors and windows.

An hour is very long on Palio day, and Giorgio was never good at waiting. The tick and the tock of the clock on the wall dawdled in maddening slowness, the hands barely moving. Every few minutes he went to the door to check the position of the sun, as if he could not trust the clock. When at last the bodyguards stirred to life, relief flooded through him. The waiting was over! It was time to dress for the pageant.

As Giorgio pulled on the blue-and-white striped stockings, the blue buskins, the quilted velvet tunic with its plaited sleeves, and the flowing wig, a curious thing happened to him. He was no longer Giorgio Terni, the peasant boy of Monticello; he was a warrior, risen full-clad from some ancient grave, ready and eager for battle.

When he arrived at the church of the Onda he saw that a change had come over Gaudenzia, too. She appeared more dazzlingly white, taller, and more elegant. She wore a spennacchiera of plumes in her headstall, and she too was adorned in medieval splendor—a blue velvet bodycloth with the dolphin embroidered almost life size in gold.

Before the arch of San Guiseppe the people stood aside. There was no talk or whispering of any kind. Solemnly they made a corridor for her and Giorgio to enter together. The mare must be blessed within the church, for is not the Palio a religious celebration in honor of the Visitation of the Virgin? Is not the blessing of the horse an age-old custom? Then, open wide the doors! Throw out the carpet. Let her enter!

In the perfect stillness, Gaudenzia's hoofbeats are the measured beat of time. Slowly she and Giorgio proceed up the aisle while the congregation breathes a collective sigh at her beauty.

Book in hand, the priest greets them at the altar. "Almighty and everlasting God," his resonant words roll out, "let this animal, Gaudenzia, receive Thy blessing, whereby it may be preserved in body, and freed from every harm by the intercession of the blessed Saint Anthony, through Christ our Lord. Amen."

Whispered "Amens" ripple through the crowd like muffled drums as the priest sprinkles holy water on Gaudenzia's head. The ceremony is over! And all at once the silence explodes in a deafening burst of joy. The clamoring rises to delirium.

Out in the street again, a tumultuous wave of humanity surrounds Gaudenzia. People from all walks of life want to touch her, or even the embroidery of her bodycloth. A man still wearing his shepherd's smock wedges himself in close to Giorgio. His face breaks into a grin, showing the dark hole where two of his teeth are missing. He points his shepherd's crook at Gaudenzia. *"Magnifica!"* he laughs in rapture.

And the crowd takes up the cry. *"Magnifica!"*

## Chapter XXIV

### HAVE YOU FEAR? HAVE YOU FEAR?

Underneath his flowing wig, perspiration is streaking down Giorgio's temples, and at the nape of his neck it trickles down and wets the ruching of his collar. The great historical pageant is about to begin, and he will be in it, and Gaudenzia will be in it. But she will walk riderless, and he will ride a mighty warhorse clad in armor of steel.

Already his contrada is forming into a tight military company—the drummer first, the two flag-bearers next with their enormous blue-and-white flags, and then Captain Tortorelli in coat-of-mail with unsheathed sword, and a major page and four minor pages. And then he, Giorgio, will come on his warhorse, and last of all Gaudenzia, led by her groom.

Giorgio's whole body is on tiptoe, on the brink of a great happening. He can feel himself growing pale, the skin of his face drawing tight over his cheekbones. A dark-bearded groom is offering his hand as a mounting block, to help him climb aboard the huge warhorse.

Giorgio stiffens. If he can mount Gaudenzia bareback, he can certainly put a foot into a stirrup and swing up without help. But the real stiffening is a feeling he has, not exactly of jealousy, but of concern that someone else is handling Gaudenzia. Will the man know how to soothe, and be firm too, amidst the jostling of people and the throb of drums, and the great race only a whisper of time away?

A nudge from the groom brings Giorgio up sharply. He waves the man aside, puts the ball of his foot on the stirrup, swings into the saddle. He feels awkward with a saddle between him and the horse—like the times he straddled a chair when he was young, and made believe it was a horse.

The groom thrusts a great iron lance into Giorgio's hand. "Hold it firm!" he warns, as he anchors it in the socket of the stirrup.

"*Attenzione!*" The Captain booms his command.

And now the whole military company moves forward, the drum beating out in somber vehemence. On both sides hundreds of people are moving with them in swirling waves, upstream toward the highest hill of Siena. Where the streets narrow, the people flatten themselves against the buildings, then come forward again, like waters rushing, receding, rushing.

Giorgio sways along on his mount like a sailor on a flat-bottom boat. The paddling gait of the warhorse is never in step with the beat of the drum; it gives him a seasick feeling. Or is the churning in his stomach a mixture of fear and joy? He glances back at Gaudenzia. She is jibbing her head, actually lifting the groom off his feet as if he were a puppet on a string. She too wants the race to start, and even now wants Giorgio's hand on her leadstrap. He feels better then, in a shamefaced way, and the seasickness leaves him.

His contrada is atop the hill now, moving past the ancient hospital where nuns and patients are craning out the windows. Before the great black-and-white Cathedral the company halts, and the flag-players fling themselves into action, paying homage to the Archbishop in a window on high. Bending, swaying, leaping over their banners, they toss their flags skyward, making the blue waves on the white silk ripple and roar like the waves of the sea.

On the wide steps of the Cathedral a great throng watches steadfast, clapping in admiration. They stand with heads uncovered to the hot July sun. Some have missed the intimate blessing within the church of their own contrada, and have come to witness this final benediction for all.

Giorgio has passed this way before, once on the war-horse of the Shell, once for the Panthers. But those other times were blurred. Then the final benediction had not seemed a direct communion from the white hand of the Archbishop way up there in the dark of the window. It had not been direct to him, but a kind of general blessing for all the contradas as they went by.

But now, on this day of July the second, 1954, Giorgio needs benediction as truly as if Time had spun back, and the year were 1260, and he was going into the Battle of Montaperti—or whatever the name of that great battle was. Now he needs the strength that the white hand up in the window can give him.

He stretches his neck, looking up, and he thinks of himself as a parched bird, head back, beak open, begging a drop of water.

There! The hand is moving. Two fingers. No, three. They are making the sign of the cross. The benediction is communion direct to him, to Giorgio Terni, and it is coming right from God, with only the Archbishop in between. Suddenly he is ready, calm and ready for battle, and he nods a little to the figure up there in the window to let him know he has received the message. His hand tightens on the lance. He sways along on his broad-backed charger and leaves the Cathedral Square; he and his whole company—the flag twirlers, and the Captain, and Gaudenzia, and all the others—and they wind down from the hill, and down, and down into the core of the city, a tight military company.

As they approach the entrance to the Piazza, the bell in the Mangia Tower begins tolling a sonorous *bong, bong, bong,* and the spine-tingling reverberations blot out all other sounds.

Before and behind are other companies. The contrada of Lupa is entering Il Campo, and Onda will be next. Yes, he will be next. And he will be really seeing the historical parade for the first time. Those other times he had moved like one in sleep. But this is real. Now he knows that the pageant is more than a parade; it is a bright fuse burning itself around the shell of Il Campo until it blazes into the fire of the Palio.

And at last, at last, he is riding into the square! His eyes blink at the awesomeness. The facades of the palaces are alive with thousands upon thousands of heads. And within the railing of the shell is a heaving sea of heads, like flowers in a pot too small—rootbound and gone riotous in bloom. And all those heads have bodies and souls, and they have come to see him and to witness battle and bravery and bloodshed; and he, Giorgio Terni, must fight off nine warriors before his white mare can capture the golden banner.

He *has* to do it because it is like keeping a promise to

himself and to those thousands of people. There are so many he dizzies trying to separate them. And all those eyes are asking for the most beautiful Palio in history, and Gaudenzia will give it to them!

The bigness of it all makes him afraid, and then he sees the small boys who have been waiting in the sun since noon, sitting there on the white posts that fence the shell. One looks up, focusing right at Giorgio with his shiny, worshipful eyes, and Giorgio knows he wants to win for him, and he wants to win for all the little *colonnini,* and for Emilio back home in Monticello, and for little boys everywhere.

At thought of home a smile crosses his face, and even through the bonging of the bell and the dinning of drums he can hear his mother say: "Giorgio Terni! Tell me! Tell me! What contrada comes first? And who next? And what happens then?"

He longs for a camera, but it would be no use. He has only two hands, and one is frozen to the lance and the other guiding the reins on a warhorse big as a battleship.

All right! He will be eyes and ears for everyone at home. His gaze moving, he peers around, taking pictures in his mind, explaining.

"Mammina! Babbo! Teria! Emilio! I have a lofty perch on my warhorse. I see across heads . . . I see the whole procession. The members of the parade are not the people of today, but what they look like—the people of long ago.

"First come the red mace-bearers stumping along tall and straight, like their maces. They make way for the black-and-white flag of Siena.

"Emilio, you should know this flag! It stands for Romulus, who founded Rome, and for Remus, who founded Siena. Like us they were brothers, only they were suckled not by a mamma, but by a she-wolf. One day those brothers build fires, and the one fire makes white smoke and the other black, and so the flag is for them . . . black and white.

"Teria! You would like better the plumed knights and nobles in their velvet costumes, and the musicians blowing on their silver trumpets.

"And Babbo! The magistrates of the guilds *you* would like—the silk workers, and wool workers, and stone and gold workers, and builders, and painters, and blacksmiths, and apothecaries."

Giorgio's eyes sharpen, dart ahead with the unbroken cavalcade as it winds triumphantly around the Piazza. How can he remember it all? How can he possibly make his family see those flag-players tossing their great flags into the air, making them soar in a hundred ways? "Oh, Mamma mia, look. Look, right now! Our boys from the Onda are doing the jump of the snowflake. Look how they leap high in the air, making the great banners unfurl, *horizontal*!

"Oh, I give up! Some day you must come. Those boys—they send their souls up with their flags into the sky. You *got* to see it. Yourself!"

Giorgio stops a moment, tired, bewildered. His brain goes blank with taking pictures, as if he has run out of film. He squirms in his saddle, forces himself on.

"Yes! All this you got to see." He tries to pick one last scene to remember, and his eyes light on the very young page boys linked shoulder-to-shoulder by green garlands. "Look, Emilio, they are no bigger than you yourself. See how they separate the ten contradas who will run from the seven who will not! And, Babbo, you would laugh how much those little boys with their loops of green look like the grapevines between our fields."

Giorgio stopped. He was out of breath. A hush had fallen over Il Campo as the parade came to an end. From the tail of his eye he saw the magnificent gold *carroccio* winding up the procession. Was this battlecar the same one as last year, and last century? He knew, of course, that it must be, but today he saw afresh the brilliant paintings on its sides, the gilded wheels, the resplendent Palio held aloft—the banner he and Gaudenzia must bring to Onda.

The hush deepened. The rolling of the drums stopped. The bonging of the bell seemed far away in the sky, but within the battlecar the silver trumpets were weaving a dialogue, the high notes calling, the low ones answering.

Giorgio straightened in his saddle. To him the high

notes were not a summons, but a question—insistent, unvaried, probing over and over and over again:

"*Have you fear? Have you fear?*"

And the silver-blown answer piercing the air:

"*Courage is the law of the Palio.*"

*Chapter XXV*

BEHOLD, THE PALIO!

Seven o'clock. Time spinning itself out. Time throwing its shadows up and up the tower. Excitement mounting with the shadows. The knights and nobles, having completed the turn of the track, seat themselves on the benches in front of the Palazzo. The rich colors of their costumes make a dazzling design, like jewels in a crown—rubies and emeralds, sapphires and amethysts.

With the other fantinos Giorgio guides his charger into the big courtyard of the Palazzo. He takes a quick look back. The track is empty now except for the flag twirlers of all the contradas. His eyes are glued to them. They look like gnomes playing with sheets of fire, flinging their furled staffs thirty feet into the air until each one bursts in a blaze of crackling color.

Before he has looked enough, the groom prods him along. "Come! Do you forget the race?"

Within the high-vaulted court all is disciplined order. Ten pages are leading the war chargers away. Ten grooms are tying their race horses to iron rings around the walls. Ten fantinos, with the help of their costume boys, are changing clothes—from suede buskins to rubber-soled shoes, from velvet tunics to cotton jackets, from plumed headgear to steel helmets. Giorgio runs his finger inside the rim of his helmet. Yes! It has been padded to fit. He sees that his hands are trembling. He wipes their dampness on a rag which the groom tosses him. He casts sidelong glances at the other fantinos. Ivan-the-Terrible glares at him, carrying on the feud from last year.

The starter picks up his megaphone, barks out rules and warnings: *"Attenzione!* It is permissible to ward off your enemy with the nerbo, but never grasp the bridle of an enemy horse. The eyes of the world are upon you. Represent well the spirit of Siena, and of your contrada. Be brave!"

Only a few minutes to go. The barbaresco of Onda carries out his final duties—checks the bridle of Gaudenzia, her cheek-strap, her chinstrap, her reins; last of all her spennacchiera . . . is it anchored solidly in case her fantino should fall? He dips his hands in a basin of water and solemnly, as if he were performing a sacred rite, uses the flat of his hands to wet the mare's withers, her back, her barrel, her flanks.

"Giorgio—" His voice sounds winded, like a run-out dog. He tries again. "Giorgio, I have made her coat damp. It will help you stick on. Now, run the best race of your life." He unties her from the iron ring. "Here, she is yours. I have done all I can. *Now rules Fate, the Queen of the Palio.*"

Giorgio takes the reins and studies the mare from pricked ears to tail. Her neck is frosted with foam, her nostrils distended, her eyes darkly intent. He does not answer the groom. He has just himself to answer. "No! No! *Not Fate!*"

Only a few seconds to go.

A squad of guards marches in, surrounds the starter to escort him to his box beneath the judges' scaffold. The man walks out slowly, his face showing worry; he knows full well that if he releases the starting rope an instant too late, ten horses may fall, and his own life be threatened by angry throngs.

The Chief-of-the-Town-Guards takes his post at the entrance of the Palazzo. In one hand he holds a white flag, in the other, ten nerbos. He looks out into the square, watches the starter mount his box, watches the ragno, the little spider-man, climb up to his cage, ready to touch off the gunpowder. He turns his head back to the courtyard. The horses and fantinos are ready.

Now! He lifts the white flag, waving it on high to alert the ragno. Bang! The air quivers as the bomb bursts in a deafening percussion. It is the signal for the fantinos to ride out. The roaring in the amphitheater stops as if cut off by a sharp knife. The silence is full of mystery, almost of pain. Then sixty thousand throats cry out:

"*A cavallo! A cavallo!* To horse! To horse!"

As each jockey in turn rides out, the Chief presents him with the nerbo. Instinctively, the horses who have been in a Palio before shy in fright.

Giorgio's breath catches in his throat. His right hand, still tingling from gripping the lance, now accepts the nerbo from the firm hands of the Chief. "Will I have to use it?" he asks himself.

Out from the maw of the courtyard the cavalcade moves forward toward the starting rope. Through his legs and thighs he can feel the mare's heart pounding against him. He hears the starter call out the horses in order. He prays for first position—or last.

"Number one, Lupa, the Wolf!" A thunder of applause goes up, boos and cheers mingling.

"Number two, the Tower!

"Aquila, the Eagle, number three!

"Tartuca, the Turtle, four!"

As they are called, the horses prance up, take their positions between the ropes. Eagle and Wolf are jumpy, move about, change positions. The starter sternly sends all four horses back, recalls them again one by one, then goes on:

"Number five, Drago, the Dragon!

"Number six, Civetta, the Owl!

"Montone, the Ram, seven!"

The whistles and the shouts are strong. "Up with Montone! Up with Montone! Up with Ivan!"

"Istrice, the Porcupine, eight!

"Giraffa, nine!"

The nine wait tensely for the final call. Giorgio tries to conceal his joy. He will be number ten! He knows the rules, revels in them. The number ten horse starts behind the others. With a rush she will come up to the rope and trigger the race.

The starter raises his megaphone. His voice shrills: "Number ten, Onda! Come on!"

Giorgio's heart beats with a wild gladness. Now it is! The time for action! He lifts Gaudenzia's head; she leaps forward. The rope drops at the split instant she touches it. It rolls free, coiling up on itself, almost onto her pasterns. As it falls to the track, ten horses are off like gunshot, Gaudenzia in the lead!

With Montone hot on her heels, she travels fast in spite of the sticky track. Landmarks spin by—the Fonte Gaia, the casino of the nobles, the palaces of Saracini and Sansedoni. Giorgio sucks in all the air his lungs can hold. Ahead lies the sharp right-angle turn of San Martino, the waiting ambulance in plain sight.

222

From bleachers, from balconies, from all over the Piazza Gaudenzia's enemies are shrieking for blood. In full stride she goes up the incline. A moment of terror! She stumbles, breaks gait. Ivan, for Montone, tries to crowd her into the posts. But Giorgio grasps her mane, squeezes his right leg into her flanks. Squeezes tighter. It works! She recovers; she's safe!

"Bravo . . . Bravissimo!" The crowd is crazed with emotion.

Only the red jacket of Montone is anywhere near as Gaudenzia flies along the straightaway to the narrows of the Casato, and uphill for the strangles of that curve. Using her tail as a rudder, she veers around the curve, gallops down the stretch to pass the starter's box, still holding the lead.

The blood sings in Giorgio's ears. He clucks to Gaudenzia for the second lap, forgets he has a nerbo. The piston legs of Montone pound on relentlessly, press forward, gain on her at the fountain, gain going around San Martino. Almost to the Casato again, Giorgio tenses, deliberately cuts in front of Ivan. He has to, to get to the rail, to shorten the distance! This is battle! All in a split second Ivan's horse is forced to prop, to brake. In turn Lupa is blocked; she swerves, careens, hurtles to the ground, dragging the oncoming Giraffa and Tartuca with her. The track is a mad scramble of horses and riders! Gaudenzia for Onda is still streaking on.

"*Forza! Forza!*" the voices shriek. "Give it to us, Giorgio! Give us the Palio!"

And around for the third time she battles Montone, who is making one last desperate effort to catch up. But he is no match for Gaudenzia. Not weaving, not wobbling, moving at a terrific pace, she goes the whole lap. As she flashes by the flag of arrival, Giorgio wildly waves his nerbo in victory. He has not used it before!

With roars of triumph, the Onda victors spill out upon the track, hug their hero, lift him up, carry him on their shoulders. Angry losers close in, to pinch and pull and buffet him. A corps of howling, happy men of Onda try to force them back, but it is the Chief-of-the-Guards who succeeds. He makes himself a one-man shield and his voice bellows like a bull. "Lift him high! *Higher!*" he commands. "Before they murder him!" Then, eyes brimming in pride, he salutes Giorgio on both cheeks, and kisses his white mare full on the mouth.

The cart horse of Casalino has won the 536th running of the Palio.

## Chapter XXVI

### VICTOR OF THE PIAZZA

It was a moment that moved the Sienese to weeping. Giorgio had never been so confused in his life; nor so happy. Here were life and glory, past and present, all in one! Up in the judges' box Captain Tortorelli was lifting the golden Palio from its socket, reaching over the railing, placing the staff in the outstretched hands of a knight from the Onda. The crowd surged toward the victory banner, then back to Giorgio as the living symbol of it. They smothered him with embraces—young men, old men, young girls, old women—frenziedly showering him with their joy. Around the square they carried him aloft on strong shoulders, first to the church to show the Palio to the image of the Virgin, then on through the streets of Siena, cheering, shouting, laughing, singing.

The little narrow alleys were packed so tight they could scarce contain the winding human river. From balconies women and children tossed red carnations to Giorgio. Catching them he thought, "These would be nice to decorate Gaudenzia's bridle. I hope she is safe from the crowd." He tried to get a glimpse of her, but she was lost in the maelstrom.

Up and down the wavy streets of Onda the growing throng marched, four abreast, six abreast, eight abreast. Young people from friendly contradas joined them. Together they invaded enemy quarters, singing their victory song, drums throbbing, hearts throbbing, flags fluttering. In enemy territory the shouts of joy were speared by catcalls. Street fighting flared up in dark doorways; old people wept tears of bitterness. But the drums never ceased, nor the singing.

A wave of pleasant tiredness washed over Giorgio. He was a piece of drift, tossed hither and yon by the seething mob as it spilled out from the canyon of walls, and overflowed into the tiny green of Lizza Park. Then all the way back down into the city again, and into the streets of the Onda.

The contrada had become a whirlpool, drawing into it friends and strangers alike. Candles twinkled like a constellation of stars. Meat, bread, watermelons, and wine appeared by magic. Bands played in the streets. Dancers swooped Giorgio into their arms. Men and women both twirled him about like a pinwheel. He ate. He drank the ceremonial wine. All night long the celebration went on, with Gaudenzia making grand appearances, her plumes nodding, her hoofs painted with gold.

At last, when the candles were guttering and the morning stars beginning to wink out, Giorgio's bodyguards rescued him and took him to his room to sleep.

Safe in his cool bed, Giorgio wanted nothing but to lie quiet in the gray darkness and live it all over again. With his eyes closed, he saw the figure of Gaudenzia rise up before him. "Look at you!" he spoke to her. "In your yesterdays you were just a poor work horse, pulling the rickety cart. Today you are . . . you are . . ." He tried to fight off sleep, to savor the deliciousness of victory, but his very bones seemed to melt into the mattress, and the shutters of his mind closed.

At eight o'clock on the morning of July third, General Barbarulli was already in the heart of the city, waiting for the newsstand to open up for business. The morning papers had just arrived, and the ancient vendor, an Ondaese, was flinging the rope-bound stacks up on the counter as if he were still giving vent to his joy. When the ropes were cut and everything was in order, he leaned toward the General, honored to have him as the first customer. "Which paper is it you would like?"

"Three of each," was the smiling reply. "One set is for the museum of Onda, one is for myself, and one for our fantino."

The transaction completed, the General stepped around the corner and went inside the post office to be less conspicuous in his enjoyment of the accounts of yesterday's victory. He stood in the light of the stained glass window and opened up the first paper. As he read, he had to hold it quite high to let his tears of happy pride fall unseen. He read all three journals, then left hurriedly to share the glowing reports with his fantino.

Giorgio was so deep in sleep that it took insistent knocking on his door to arouse him. The bodyguards, exhausted from the celebration, still lay bundled in their sheets, snoring softly. Giorgio quickly pulled on his shirt and trousers and stepped out into the hallway.

"My boy," the General smiled broadly, "you have a new name!" Tapping Giorgio lightly on the shoulder with the newspapers, he spoke in staccato excitement.

"Read! Read, now! These stories you will want to send home to Monticello." He spread out the front pages of each paper on the hall table and stood waiting to see the effect they would have.

Giorgio read slowly, struggling over some of the longer words. "The fantino of the Onda," the first article said, "who last year found difficulty in securing a mount, this year has won everlasting recognition from the people of the Onda, who carried him aloft in triumph. The Palio, in the midst of a sea of flags, has already made its entrance into the museum of the contrada. The little hero of the Piazza . . ." He blushed, embarrassed to go on.

"Read more—read more," the General urged. "The Palio has christened you! You have a new name. Look! See for yourself."

Giorgio read faster now, skimming as best he could. What was wrong with the name he had? What was wrong with Giorgio Terni? The second paper said nothing about a name. He turned to the third and read, "Young Giorgio Terni, peasant boy from the Maremma, is now crowned with a new name. Sienese everywhere speak of him as *Vittorino*, the little victor of the Piazza."

Giorgio's heart quickened. Maybe some people would call "Vittorino" a nickname, he thought, but to me it seems a very nice title.

"The battle was not as fierce as expected," the article went on. "The fantinos did not use their nerbos, for

Gaudenzia was first from beginning to end. The masterful performance of horse and rider together has given the youngest fantino in the Palio his new name. Henceforth he will be known as Vittorino."

"Vit-to-ri-no!" the boy tasted it on his tongue.

General Barbarulli beamed. "It pleases you? No?"

"Si, si! It is better than *Professore* or *Dottore* or even . . ." the boy reddened.

"Better even than *Generale*?" the General's eyes twinkled. "I agree! It is a beautiful laurel, invisible, to wear with honor and pride. And now we have many weeks for rejoicing." He sighed happily as he folded his own newspapers. "Then in September, when nights are cool, we will hold our Victory Dinner right in the middle of Via Giovanni Du Pré. A thousand places will be set under the stars, and Gaudenzia will be the guest of honor. At the head table she will be served! And you, Vittorino, can feast your eyes and your stomach without even making a speech. It will be your and Gaudenzia's grand triumph. Now, then, I have much to see about and must be on my way."

He shook hands briskly, turned on his heel, and went lightly down the stairs.

*Chapter XXVII*

A TIME TO SEEK

The next weeks that should have been all gay and rejoicing for a hero of the Piazza turned dark with worry. It concerned Gaudenzia, and yet it didn't concern her. The August Palio was less than six weeks away, but already Giorgio felt troubled by a thing he did not understand. Suppose another fantino should ride her then, and he would have to fight against her!

He tried to argue with himself. "Look here, Giorgio, in your pocket you have some money. In the streets children salute you with flags. In the Palazzo Pubblico men

231

treat you man-sized. And every day you receive poems, presents, and pictures. Yet you are not happy."

Deliberately he turned all his attention on the mare. He would keep her stall cleaner than a kitchen, and her mantle spotless. And if he worked on a new training program for her, he might be too busy to worry.

This time he did not bother with a calendar. He had only to ease her off from the pinnacle of July second, then build her right back up again.

The Chief-of-the-Guards was too happy to notice how silent Giorgio had grown. He lived in a state of blissful pride, for Gaudenzia seemed in no way weakened by racing on the treacherous course.

"If anything, she is now more strong," he said time and again. "Legs firm and trim. No puffy swellings around the joints. No cuts from overreaching or crossfiring. And no bruising or splitting of her hoofs. As for the corners of her mouth, they are soft like a young filly's. Who could recognize her as the sad bag-of-bones we rescued from the sausage maker. Eh, son?"

The Chief was aware that other contradas would now want the famous Vittorino to ride for them, but his contrada, Nicchio, had asked first. He refused to think that in the next battle the boy might have to ride another horse and so fight against Gaudenzia. Surely, whoever drew Gaudenzia would buy Giorgio from the Nicchio.

Giorgio, however, did not have this assurance. And

whenever he tried to voice his fears, the Chief seemed so happy that the words died unspoken.

But if the boy had grown broody and silent, Gaudenzia was just the opposite. She felt intensely alive. Let out of her stable, she tried to rake the sky for sheer joy in living. She felt good! Never was she alone, not even on rainy days; her fantino was groom and companion, too, steadfast as the earth. And so she thrived.

From fast work she went to slower and longer work. She walked and trotted one week, two weeks. Then gradually Giorgio intensified her training. More trotting and galloping, less walking. More grain, less hay.

"For you, your life will always be mountains and valleys," he told her one morning as they jogged along a country byway. "Always between Palios comes the easing off, the nice rest. Then you must start all over again and make the steep climb to new peaks."

A fluffy seed blew into her nose. She blew it out again with a loud snort.

"Yes, you can snort away your little troubles. But me?" Sighing, he ran his eye along the distance, along the tufted terraces of olive gardens, and he followed the aerial maneuvers of a pair of swallows snapping insects on the wing. By keeping his mind busy he hoped to wear blinders to what was bothering him. But it was no use. The worry kept eating at his heart. Maybe he would feel better if he put it into words, instead of letting it run around in his head like a mouse in a mill.

"Listen, Gaudenzia," he spoke into the fine pricked ears, "for one little month you are Queen of the Palio. But you won your crown without . . ."

His talk sounded silly against the shimmer of distance. He clucked to the mare. A faster pace might make the words come faster, easier.

He tried again to make his voice strong, to empty his thoughts. "Gaudenzia! You won the July Palio without real battle, without the nerbo, without the secret arrangements." The words flowed faster. "Now you are marked. You are the one to beat. You and I—in the next Palio we could be separated. The contrada which draws you could already have engaged some other fantino." He burst out shouting: "What if you have to be beaten and slashed back? By me!"

The sweat broke cold on his face. He pulled the mare to a halt, and she stood trembling at his tone as if already she were beaten over the head with his nerbo. Thinking of her nervous tic, he quickly dismounted and quieted her.

July passed. Giorgio had no peace. His dream of the Palio had become sullied. He called on the Chief-of-the-Guards in his own home. He called on General Barbarulli. He sought out Signor Ramalli. With each he tried to unburden his worry, but the talk was round-about and never came near the sore spot.

In desperation, one day, he put Gaudenzia in the care of a barbaresco and went home to Monticello. He

planned to arrive in the late afternoon, when he knew
his mother would be cooking supper. She would be
standing in the pool of light from the single bulb over
the stove, and her back would be toward him, and the
room would be steamy warm, and in the semi-darkness
it would be easy to speak right out.

It happened exactly like that. Giorgio was there in
the kitchen, leaning against the wall where the patched
green umbrella hung, and both cats were sidling up
against his legs as if they remembered him from yesterday, and he was saying, "Mamma, now that I am grown,
the Palio is a thing I do not understand."

His mother was making pizzas, shaping each pie carefully. She stood there in her black dress and did not turn around. And yet Giorgio felt her motherliness spread over him like wings over a young bird.

"Giorgio," she began, then corrected herself. "My boy is now Vittorino. He has the wished-for name, and in his keeping he has the wished-for mare. Yet he does not understand the workings of the Palio, and so he is unhappy."

"That is the way of it, Mamma."

"You are not alone in this, Vittorino. Many things of history *I* do not understand. Nor does your Babbo. But the part that torments you, maybe it is a thing to pull out of the dark and into the light. Maybe then . . ."

She stopped short, choosing silence for urging the boy on.

Giorgio blurted out: "Mamma! It is the secret arrangements between the contradas. The Palio is a religious festival. Is it right, do you think, to hold your horse back, to make her lose? What if"—the words came tight and strained—"what if for Gaudenzia another fantino should be chosen? And I should have to strike her?"

The shaping of the pies went on in silence.

"I had to ask it! Everyone in Onda is happy. And the Chief is happy. And Gaudenzia is happy. But I, I am sad! Some nights, for hours I do not sleep. How can I be a fantino so soon again if in my heart there is a heaviness? How can I?"

The mother sighed deeply. Why is it, she thought, that always children have questions like knots which they throw into the lap of the mother? Little children, little knots; big children, big knots. Always it is so. She thought a long time and the room grew so still that the whir of a hummingbird at a flower in the window sounded big and loud.

"I think there is someone," she said at last, "who could ease your burden."

Giorgio was hearing with every fiber. "Tell me! Who is it?"

The mother seemed to be talking to herself, convincing herself. "Yes! He would be the one; he is wise in the mysteries that trouble the heart."

"Who, Mamma?"

"He is a thoughtful, listening man."

"But who *is* he?"

"He knows especially boys; he believes they deserve to be heard."

"But *who*?" It was a cry for help.

"His name," the mother said with a little glow of wonder, "his name is Monsignor Tardini."

"Monsignor Tardini!"

"Si."

"Why, he is a great man at the Vatican. He stands next to the Pope himself!"

The mother went to the cupboard and took out plates and cups to set the table. "Soon now the pizzas will be done," she said, "and Babbo and the children will come from the farm, and we eat."

"But why does the Monsignore understand especially boys?"

"Because, in a pine grove on the skirts of Rome, there sits a beautiful villa for orphans. It is called Villa Nazareth, and Monsignor Tardini, he is the guiding spirit. Even the grown boys, after they go out into the world, bring their troubles to him."

"But, Mamma, how do you know all this?"

"I know because young Arturo, a boy from the Maremma, is there. *He* says so."

"You mean I should go all the way to Rome? To the Vatican?"

The mother nodded. "You should go, even if it costs dear. In the sugar bowl there is money. Yours and Gaudenzia's," she smiled, "from the victory of Onda." She stopped to pinch off a few faded flowers from the pots in the window. Then she went back to the stove. "There comes a time," she said, turning to look right at Giorgio, "when to make a pilgrimage is necessary for peace of the mind."

A far look crept into the boy's eyes. Suddenly he burned with the urge to go to Rome.

*Chapter XXVIII*

ALL ROADS LEAD TO ROME

Two days later, back in Siena, Giorgio dressed at dawn and went to say good-bye to Gaudenzia. She gazed steadfastly at him as if he had made the morning sunbeams slant westward for the day, as if he had made the grain she ate, and the air she breathed. "Do not have fear," he told her. "I return *presto, pronto, subito.* I return this night."

Already he felt better. The mere prospect that today he could unburden his worries was like strength in his blood. He filled Gaudenzia's hayrack and water pail. He stripped her stall of bedding and swept the floor. He brought in sheaves of bright straw and shook them and padded them and banked them around the walls.

A friendly groom came in as he was putting the fork away. The man was big and brawny with sad, red-rimmed eyes like a hound dog's. He clapped Giorgio on the back.

*"Ah, Roma! Bella, bella Roma!"* he sighed, rolling his eyes heavenward and kissing his fingertips. "My favorite of cities! You will see the catacombs and the Colosseum and the Castle of San Angelo. But why," he puzzled, "do you go *now* when the manifestation of the Palio already makes the air crackle?"

"I cannot explain. I must hurry. Soon my train leaves. Please, Signore, kindly do me the favor to look in on Gaudenzia twice before nightfall."

The seven o'clock train chugged out of the station at the exact stroke of seven. Giorgio, his hair combed so carefully the teeth marks showed, sat in a second-class compartment filled with soldiers sleeping. They paid him less attention than if he had been a fly. He was glad. He could read again the exciting note in his pocket.

"The Right Reverend Monsignor Tardini," it said, "will see you at the Vatican at twelve-thirty on Thursday next." And it was signed, "Angelina Ciambellotti, leader of work with children, Siena."

Having nothing to do, he read the few words again

and admired the signature of this woman he hardly knew. The pen strokes were strong and sure. Did she ever worry about things, he wondered; or was her path laid out straight as a piece of string? Maybe working for orphans as she and the Monsignore did was like holding a compass in the hand; always you knew the way. He folded the letter and put it back in his pocket, alongside the light race shoe of Gaudenzia which he was taking as a gift for the Monsignore. His fingers closed about it for comfort.

The soldiers were still sleeping, grunting and twitching as if they fought imaginary battles. Giorgio wished he could sleep, too, but he had never before been to Rome and he might miss the junction at Chiusi where he had to change to an express. When he finally reached it he was in a panic for fear he would get on the wrong train. He asked a dozen people to make sure.

"You have much time," they laughed. "Why not have a coffee?"

Remembering now that he had forgotten to eat breakfast, he gulped a tiny cup of coffee and bought a sugared roll. When at last the express to Rome roared into the station, he crowded in with the others and found a seat beside a gangling American student.

The rest of the trip was a succession of dark tunnels and hairpin curves, of haystacks and strawstacks, and boys herding sheep, and oxen pulling plows between rows of grain.

Calmer now, Giorgio leaned back against the high cane seat. The train went no farther than Rome, so he closed his eyes and let the flowing countryside and the warm August air lull him to sleep.

It was the young American who, tugging at Giorgio's sleeve, woke him up. "All roads lead to Rome!" he said in Italian with a strong American accent. "We are here!"

Giorgio thanked him and burst out of the train. He hadn't meant to sleep. Suppose he had overslept and missed his appointment with the Monsignore! He ran through the station, skirting a big bed of pansies, darting his way through the surge of people, past the food and drink vendors, past porters trundling mountains of baggage. Out in the street he stopped a policeman.

"The Vatican!" he gasped. "Monsignor Tardini, he awaits me!"

The policeman smiled, then laughed. "Is it *urgente*?"

"*Si, si! Urgente!*"

The white-gloved hand made a wide circle in the air. "My boy," he bowed, "to go by carriage is best. Then the sights you see, and quickly you get there, too."

Nearby, the driver of a carriage, a sparrowy man with a tall hat, dropped his newspaper and was at Giorgio's side in an instant. "For one thousand lire I take you to the Vatican," he offered.

"One thousand lire!"

Suddenly the driver saw in the young boy a pilgrim come to the Holy City, a boy all alone with trouble. A strange resemblance to his own grandson made him say, "Jump up! You sit here beside me. We fly together." He waved Giorgio onto the high front seat, slapped the lines over the rump of a bony mare, cracked his whip, and the cart took off with Giorgio sitting alongside the grinning driver.

Up and down the streets of the great city the gaunt creature clattered at a lively pace. The time clock in her head told her it was almost time for the nosebag. The sooner she delivered her passenger, the sooner she could plunge her muzzle into a bagful of cut-up greens. Onlookers laughed and cheered them on as if they were in a race. Nearing St. Peter's Square, the driver tried to pull her down to a sedate walk, but she was no respecter of religion. And so, lathered and blowing, she swung at breakneck speed through the gates of the Holy City.

The wide piazza of St. Peter's with its obelisk and gushing fountains was alive with movement—nuns sailing in their starchy wimples, priests billowing in black robes, sailors and soldiers and pilgrims from everywhere clicking cameras, feeding the pigeons, gazing up at the great dome of the church.

The driver pulled up in front of the basilica. He shook hands with Giorgio as with an old friend. "Boy," he directed, "that way you go! No, not up the center to the church. To the right wing! Up the steps and through the bronze portal. To you I wish best luck; and now, *arrivederci,* my son."

Inside the grilled door two Swiss Guards, resplendent in striped livery, blocked Giorgio's entrance with their halberds.

"I—I—" Giorgio stuttered miserably. He was no longer Vittorino, the brave fantino who had won the July Palio. He was only Giorgio, shrinking in size, getting littler and littler until once again he was the runt of Monticello. Suddenly he thought of the letter in his pocket and presented it to the imposing guard, wrong side up.

Unsmiling, the man turned it around, read the single sentence carefully, and with a formal nod motioned him inside the Papal palace.

Afterward Giorgio never remembered how many footmen in gray and how many officials in black and how many Palatine guards read the letter and said, "Come this way," or "Go that way." Nor did he remember how many frescoed passages he walked, nor how many glass-enclosed elevators he rode, nor how many grand staircases and minor staircases he climbed. He moved as one in a dream, through marble halls, and around and around, and up and up and up, until he found himself in a magnificent courtyard open to the sky. He crossed its immensity, feeling antlike beside the gigantic statues of the apostles towering above him. Then he was ushered into an empty chamber that seemed a trinket in size, yet was more beautiful than any he had ever known.

"You may be seated," the guide said, and disappeared.

Perching gingerly on the edge of a settee, Giorgio felt less secure than if he were riding bareback on a runaway horse. He mopped his brow and folded his handkerchief. He looked about him. The room was all red and gold. The gold chairs were covered in a rosy red, like the colors worn by the Ram in the Palio. And the walls were the same rosy red.

Everything was quiet. Occasional wisps of conversation drifted in, but these only emphasized the stillness. For a moment he wanted to bolt. He knew now how Gaudenzia felt when left all alone, with no familiar hands or voice.

And just when the silence grew terrifying, a young

clerk beckoned him across the hall and into a room with half-closed shutters. It was pleasantly dark and cool. "The Monsignore will see you now," the young man said.

And there, coming to meet Giorgio, was Monsignor Domenico Tardini, Pro-secretary of State for Extraordinary Affairs.

Giorgio looked up at him, tongue-tied. The face was all faces in one—kindly and penetrating, old and very young, smiling and stern—and the eyes, dark and deep-set behind the thick glasses, were both fiery and serene.

Seeing the worry in Giorgio's face, the Monsignore waved him kindly to a row of chairs against the wall, and he himself pulled one out and sat facing the boy.

"I congratulate you," he began with a gentle smile. "Signora Ciambellotti has informed me about you. It is a happy occasion to salute a new star of the Palio."

Giorgio could not answer; he only gulped.

The Monsignore went on, talking more to himself than to the boy. "Vittorino," he spoke the name slowly, elegantly, precisely. "'Victory of the Small One,' it means. I have many boys at Villa Nazareth who look upon you as their hero. To ride in the Palio is to them like riding through the gates of heaven.

"Now," he said, running his hands through his short-cropped hair, "I am truly glad you came. You see, today there are affairs of state which prevent me from going out to visit those boys. But you have come to see me in their stead. Even in their sheltered life they have many problems. Do you, too, have a problem?"

"Monsignore?"

"Yes, my son."

Giorgio plunged one hand into his pocket and his fingers clutched the thin horseshoe. "Do you have enough time for me? With affairs of state and all?"

"As much as you need. You see," he smiled, "I am in charge of extraordinary affairs, and this just might be an extraordinary affair."

"It is!" Giorgio sat up straighter, and suddenly the floodgates opened. "Monsignore! In the Palio of August the Contrada of Nicchio might not draw Gaudenzia."

"And why is it you wish Nicchio to draw her?"

"Because they asked me last year to ride for them."

"Then why did you ride for Onda in July?"

"Because then Nicchio was one of the seven contradas that did not run."

"Ah, yes. Of course. So it is one chance in ten that your mare should be assigned to Nicchio?"

The boy nodded. And again his questions flew like arrows to a target. "Monsignore! The Palio is a religious festival. Why then is it right for the captains to make the secret agreements? Why is it right for the fantinos to help other horses win and hold back their own? Why is it?"

The voices out in the halls faded away. The room seemed to contract. There were just the two of them—the

247

man thinking, and the boy with the eager hope in him, sitting . . . watching . . . waiting out his answer.

"It is an honest question, Vittorino"—the words came slowly—"and only half the answer do I know."

"Yes?"

"Suppose we turn back some pages into history. Suppose we remember that before the year 1721 all seventeen contradas were allowed to race. Is not that true?"

"Si, si."

"The course is very narrow, is it not, Giorgio?"

"Si."

"When all seventeen raced, how was the departure from the starting rope?"

"Monsignore! How could they all get away at once?"

"They couldn't! Some fell and were trampled. So now the contradas draw lots for the honor of competing, and only ten horses run. Is not that better for the horse?"

"Oh, si."

"And the people do not wager any money on the race. That is good, no?"

Giorgio nodded, wishing the Monsignore would get to the core.

"And now mattresses are placed upright about the dangerous curves to protect horses and fantinos both. Is that not better than in days of old when heads of man and beast cracked against the walls?"

"Si!"

"And the contrada that wins makes nothing, but spends much. Is not that so?"

"It is."

"And at their banquets the rich and the poor, the rulers and the workers sit at table in happy contact, and no one feels diminished or humiliated. Is it not good?"

"It is."

"But if a contrada draws a poor horse, then it can try to help a friendly contrada? Is that so?"

Giorgio winced. "That is the part! That is it! What if I have to hinder Gaudenzia? She will not understand. A whole year now she trusts in me. On her open cuts I put salt and alum. Under her belly she lets me walk to sew her blanket in place. It is me who nursed and trained her."

The Monsignore knew he had touched the sore spot. He tried to put himself in the boy's place. "Can you get along without being a fantino? Can you live without taking part in this Palio, and the next, and . . ."

"No, no, Monsignore," Giorgio interrupted. "Ever since I was a little boy, there is no other world for me."

"Then, my son, what your captain tells you to do, that you must do. The Palio is war. Contradas form alliances as countries do, to help each other fight a common enemy."

Giorgio sat silent at the desolating words.

"But of course"—the Monsignore took off his spectacles, and now he spoke eagerly, earnestly—"the unforeseen can happen! Have you forgotten," he asked, "the grand element of uncertainty? The horse knows nothing of the clouds of intrigue gathering while he eats happily his grain. He knows only that he is the servant of man, who sometimes betrays him."

The Monsignore had not finished. His gaze went past the boy's head, through the walls and beyond. "Perhaps that is why the humble St. Francis of Assisi wished to be Protector to Animals."

His eyes then came back to Giorgio and flashed warmly. "As fantino, you must know that the probability of winning the Palio is based on the speed of the horse, the skill of the fantino, and the diplomacy of the captain. But it cannot be said that even with all these favorable, the victory is secure. Man tries to fix and arrange, but ah, the horse . . . he knows only the one law, and that is to win. It is the most beautiful and bittersweet lesson of the Palio."

A young clerk came into the room and placed a sheaf of papers on the desk. Giorgio sensed that affairs of state were piling up.

"It is not a whole answer, my son," the Monsignore concluded, "but it is the best I can do."

Giorgio stood up to go. Already he began to breathe more easily, as if something of the great man's spirit had passed over into him. "Thank you," he said quietly. Then he pressed the horseshoe into the blue-veined hands, kissed them both and fled from the room.

*Chapter XXIX*

THE THREE ACTS

That evening when Giorgio returned to Siena, the undercurrent of the August Palio was running strong. The first act, the drawing of lots of the contradas, had already taken place, and the flags of the ten who would run were flying from the Palazzo Pubblico. As Giorgio stood in the Piazza looking, the torment in him began again. If only by some miracle the flag with the sea-shell were missing, then whichever contrada drew Gaudenzia would surely ask him to race her. But of course, the flag was there, as he knew it had to be, and he was bound irretrievably to Nicchio, the Shell.

Feeling trapped and helpless, he hurried at once to the stable to see how Gaudenzia had fared. She was always a surprise to him each time he saw her, always belonging to him more closely—the pricked ears listening, the dark eyes asking, the nostrils fluttering in a welcome that said more than any words.

"See!" he said quite out of breath, "I come *presto, pronto, subito*. For you, too, was this day endless like eternity?" He let the mare lip his shirtsleeve, not minding the warm wetness nor the greenish tint from the hay she'd been munching. "I got to tell you," he said soberly, "there is now only one chance in ten you will have me for fantino in the August Palio. If Nicchio does not draw you . . ." He turned away and grabbed a pitchfork with both hands. The mare was already bedded for the night, but with slow, forceful motions he shook up and freshened the straw. Then he waited until she buckled her knees and lay down in contentment before he left her and went to his own bed.

The days until the Palio were cut to a pattern and moved on schedule. Seven days before, the workmen dumped cartloads of yellow-red earth and tamped it down on the track. Four days before, carpenters put up tier upon tier of seats in front of the palace buildings, and the chest-high railing to fence the spectators within the shell.

Three days before came the second big act of the

Palio—the trials to determine which horses were strong and stout enough to negotiate the course. The day was clear, the air still fresh with morning. An expanding crowd was filling up the newly erected seats. There was no shrieking or yelling yet. The people were murmuring, waiting.

At the express wish of the Chief-of-the-Guards, Giorgio rode Gaudenzia in the trials. Again he held her in, and again she obeyed, acting almost sedate in her performance. Some of the new horses shied at the ropes, were afraid to enter between them, and some lurched and sprawled at the hairpin curves. And so the heats, in batteries of five, had to be run again and again until the judges were ready to make their decisions. Then behind closed doors the secret voting took place while the fantinos waited tensely in the court of the Palazzo and the crowd in the Piazza began chanting for the favorites:

"Give us U-gan-da!"

"Give us Gau-den-zia!"

"Give us Pin-noc-chio!"

At last a deputy stepped importantly into the courtyard with a page at heel like a well-trained dog. At a command from the deputy, the page took numbered discs from a box and fastened one on the cheekstrap of each of the ten horses chosen. At the moment he fastened the number 6 on Gaudenzia's bridle, a horseboy took hold of her reins. He almost had to pry Giorgio's hands loose. "Let go!" he said in annoyance. "Let go!"

Giorgio, with the other fantinos, was ordered into the Piazza. They stood shoulder to shoulder in front of the long table with the two urns on it. Three times he had witnessed this third act before the Palio—the assignment of the horses. Three times he had watched twin pageboys draw the wooden capsules from the urns. Three times he had watched the Mayor's hands tremble and the captains' faces pale.

And three times he had stood in this same strip of shade made by the Mangia Tower, with the ten grooms in front of him, waiting to lead away their charges in joy or sorrow, and behind him the anxious contradaioli, repeating the phrase he had grown to hate: *"Fate is Queen of the Palio."*

Like the Mayor himself, Giorgio was beginning to tremble. Not just his hands; he was shaking all over. Perspiration trickled freely down his back as the capsules were opened and the pairing began.

"Uganda to the Snail!"

The clamor was loud in Giorgio's ears, growing with each announcement.

"Dorina to the Panther!" Poor Dorina, he thought, always running, never winning.

"Gaudenzia to the Giraffe!"

"Rosella to Nicchio, the Shell!"

Giorgio had heard all he needed to hear. The capsules had sealed his doom. A horrified gasp broke from his throat. It was the same sound he had made when he hit the cobblestones with Turbolento.

The ritual of the assignment went on. But for Giorgio it was over. It was done.

He watched Rosella and Gaudenzia going off with their grooms, each surrounded by joyful contradaioli. The spectators, too, were melting away—going home, going into cafés, returning to work. The captains and the Mayor vanished into the communal hall. Only Giorgio and the pigeons were left. And in a silent semi-circle behind him three tall youths from Nicchio had taken up their positions as his bodyguards. He turned to them. In a daze he shook their hands, and in a daze smiled crookedly at their small talk. The pigeons, in their pigeon-toed gait, waddled around them. He envied the birds, earthbound one moment, soaring into sky the next. He reached into his pocket and scattered a few kernels of oats, and watched the airborne ones come in for a landing. One perched on his shoulder, eyeing him with a shiny shoe-button eye.

"Our fantino, he thinks he is St. Francis!" a guard laughed, not unkindly.

Giorgio remembered the time Emilio had said almost the same words, and suddenly he longed to be at home in the two little rooms in Monticello. Forlornly, he followed the guards to his new sleeping room in the quarters of Nicchio. He had half a mind to steal out tonight and go back to the Maremma, but if he did, it would be only his body that left.

The Captain of Nicchio, Signor de Santi, came later in the afternoon to see him. For a moment Giorgio felt a spear of hope. Perhaps Giraffa and Nicchio had exchanged fantinos, and the Captain had come with the news.

It was a cruel hope, dashed almost as it was born. Sensing the boy's unhappiness, the Captain said, "Son, you are a fantino, not a mere horseboy. On this mount, or that, you must win. Rosella is a big, rangy mare and she, too, has good possibilities."

Giorgio made no answer. Empty of feeling, he managed to live out the afternoon. Toward evening the Chief-of-the Guards came to him. "It will be some comfort," he said, "for you to ride Gaudenzia tonight in the first Prova. Of course, you understand," he added, "it will be in this one only."

But it was no comfort at all. It was like digging at

a wound so that it could bleed anew. He let Gaudenzia win the first Prova, lengths ahead of the others. No one had challenged her.

On the morning of the second day he rode the rangy Rosella. Captain de Santi gave his orders beforehand. "Make the getaway clear from the ropes, and the gallop light. In all the Provas, her strength and vigor must be preserved."

Time passed for Giorgio. The minutes and the hours flowed on, sunup to sundown, one Prova after another, and the pinch of pain spread until it was a dull, dull aching.

In the Prova Generale, on the afternoon of the third day, tension tightened among the fantinos. Each wanted to show his skill, to make certain of being selected for the Palio itself. In July, Giorgio had been tortured by the fear that his name would not be made official in the archives. Now it did not matter. Again he brought Rosella in safely, as his captain had ordered.

That evening, escorted by his bodyguard, he attended the great banquet in the hall of Nicchio. Wearing the little jacket and the striped trousers of the race, he sat at the head table, next to Captain de Santi. There was joy and hospitality all about him . . . people eating their fill of chicken cacciatore and drinking the red wine from the grapes of Tuscany. He tried to be one of them, but he was silent as a nut in a shell, and the good food knotted in his throat. In his mind he saw Monsignor Tardini in the cool, shuttered room of the Vatican, and he saw the Umbrella Man sitting cross-legged at the fountain, and he saw Gaudenzia without wanting to see her.

When it came his turn to stand up and face the members of Nicchio, he did not fumble in his mind or in his pocketless jacket for any prepared speech. He just got up and stood quiet awhile. Then, remembering his talk with the Monsignore, he said: "To Nicchio I will be loyal." It was as if another's voice were speaking for him as he went on, "And the orders of my Captain I will obey."

*Chapter XXX*

## DUEL BETWEEN HORSE AND MAN

The hours of night flowed over Giorgio's sleeping room. He and his guards were trying to settle down, but each heart was groping alone in the dark, wondering which contrada would win tomorrow's Palio.

Giorgio knew that somewhere in remote and quiet places throughout the city the captains were meeting in secret, making their agreements, planning their strategy. Overnight the whole aspect of the Palio could change. And tomorrow, he thought with a surge of hope, Captain de Santi will come to me and say: "We of Nicchio generally live in a state of neutrality. But last night we formed an alliance with Giraffa. Therefore, your precise order in today's joust is to hinder the others and help our ally to win. Since they have drawn Gaudenzia, you are fortunate, thus, to fight for your mare. No?"

Or, better still, the Captain might say: "Vittorino! In the dark watches of the night we changed our tactics. Our Rosella, it appears, could finish maybe second or third, but not first. Therefore, we release you to ride Gaudenzia for Giraffa, and we will engage a new fantino."

In Giorgio's mind the Captain's speech grew long and lofty. "You see, son," (he could even hear the tone of voice) "Giraffa has in the past done us favors. We therefore hold in high esteem their sacred friendship. It will be a beautiful sacrifice we make."

Hugging these hopes to him, he slept away what was left of the night.

August 16, 1954. The day is new. Sky murky. Sun trying to tear the clouds apart. Church bells tolling. Giorgio cannot run away now; does not want to run away. There is still the hope. He prays with the other fantinos, feels with them the pressure and the tension mounting. He rides in the *Provaccia,* the last rehearsal. Bodily he is on Rosella; heart and soul he rides Gaudenzia. Last night's hopes will come true; *must* come true! Perhaps at the last moment in the Hall of the Magistrate it will happen. Captain de

Santi will lean over and whisper into his ear. He can do it easily. The hall is vast; two people can feel alone.

But when the time came, there was no whispering; only the bold pronouncement that Giorgio Terni, known as *Vittorino,* was official fantino for Nicchio.

At half past two in the afternoon the embers of his hope flickered again as the Captain strode into Giorgio's room.

"Vittorino!" The name slow-spoken as in the dream, and the syllables far apart, like drops of rain when the storm begins.

Now it comes. Now he will say: "You, Vittorino, must give help to Gaudenzia. The others you will block. With the nerbo you will fight them fiercely, hinder them." The boy holds his breath. He takes a step closer. He does not want even the guards to overhear. He cants his head like a dog, begging, awaiting directions . . . listening . . . eyes beseeching.

The Captain clips out his orders, *wanting* the guards to hear: "Break first from the rope! The hot bludgeons of the nerbo we wish you both to escape."

There is still the hope; it is not yet dead.

"And during the last meters of the race"—the voice is grim—"you will nerbo every opponent who threatens our victory. *Every* opponent who threatens . . ."

A wild sickness churns in the boy. He wants to escape and run and run and run, but where to go? Fate has trapped him. Fate, the Queen of the Palio.

Minutes and seconds wear themselves out. Numbly he puts on the long stockings, the high buskins, the deep blue doublet with the emblem of the white shell, the burnished sleeves of mail, the heavy helmet of mail with the chinstrap too tight. He thinks wistfully of the rabbit's fur he had once wrapped around Gaudenzia's chinstrap. How long ago that seems!

He is ready. He goes to the church of Nicchio with Rosella. He hears the priest invoke God's protection for horse and rider, hears the people shout: "Go, Rosella! Come back victorious!"

Then, mounted on his parade horse, he receives the general blessing of the Archbishop, his mind dazedly repeating the Captain's orders. He makes his way to Il Campo, awaits his turn to enter. The bell in the tower begins its tolling. His company moves forward. He enters the square, sees again the many-headed multitude in the shallow basin of the Piazza. He thinks: "So solid are they packed one could walk across their heads without having to leap."

His mind and body are far apart. No longer does he want to be a Sienese. He is an intruder, belonging neither to the present nor to the past, but suspended in time. Staring hopelessly, he watches the figures of the pageant move around the Piazza like wooden people on wooden horses on a merry-go-round. He sees the mare Gaudenzia, proud-headed. She is the only white one, the only Arabian. He feels a moment of pride.

Then the flags cut her off from sight and the numbness clutches him again, and the merry-go-round figures go on and on until his head dizzies with looking. At sight of the four great oxen pulling the gilded battlecar, he sighs in welcome relief. The merry-go-round is at last coming to a stop.

The sun, too, is completing its orbit, shedding a soft light over Il Campo. The multitude waits. Inside the courtyard Giorgio wants an end to things. It seems a hundred hours, a hundred days, a hundred years since the fateful orders were imposed. All right, then, let's go. Change costumes! Put on the little jacket, the coarse pants. Eye your opponents. Swing up, bareback. Take the hard nerbo in your hard hand. Line up! Remember, it's war! Contrada against contrada! Not rider, not mount, not flesh and blood, but symbols . . . Eagle against Owl, Dragon against Panther, Snail against Wave, Giraffe against me.

All right, then. Touch off the gunpowder! Let the flame belch! Let the deafening percussion jar the ancient stones loose. Let the starter spring the rope.

It is happening! Now!

Ten horses bursting into life, breaking from the ropes. Together! Ten horses like a sudden blast of wind. But look! The swirling gust is breaking apart, three horses striking through—two browns, one white. The browns are the Snail and the Wave, the white is Gaudenzia. Under a hail of blows the three in the lead round the easy curve beyond the Fonte Gaia, begin their drive to the death-jaws of San Martino.

Sixty thousand throats shriek in horror. The Snail and the Wave are heading crazedly for a crash. They collide! Two fantinos are spewed into the air, go rolling ahead like tumbleweeds. Gaudenzia's rider pulls her back, swerves her sharp around the bodies. She's in first place!

Coming up from behind, Giorgio snakes Rosella between the riderless horses, takes the curve, catches Gaudenzia on the straightaway, passes her.

Did her nostrils pull in his scent as he went by? Did her ears pull in his voice? If not, why is she jibbing her head; why is she weaving at the lesser curve of the Casato? Tiring? She can't be! Not on the first round with the whole width of the curve to herself.

For endless seconds she is unpredictable. Then she rears up, savagely rakes the air, deliberately tosses her fantino! She's free! With a wild spurt she tries to catch Giorgio. The duel between horse and man is on!

*"Attento! Attento!"* Nicchio fans are screaming in frenzy, imploring Giorgio: "Give it to us! Give us the Palio!"

But who knows the mind of a horse? Is some inner urge compelling Gaudenzia to spend all of her fleetness and blood? Is the thunder and ecstasy of the crowd like fierce music in her ears? Who can know?

For the entire second round she battles Giorgio for

the lead, catching him on the straightaways, thundering alongside him, only to drop back when he blocks her at the curves.

"*Forza*, Gaudenzia! *Forza!*" Strangers and Sienese alike are yelling for Gaudenzia.

Only the Nicchio fans are her enemies. "Knock off her spennacchiera!" they cry to Giorgio. "Knock it off!"

Fifty meters to go! She is holding her own, pounding on, eye to eye with Rosella.

In sickening guilt Giorgio remembers his orders . . . lifts his nerbo, aims at her spennacchiera. He misses! He feels the thud of his blow against her neck. She falls back a moment, but immediately comes up again. Desperately aiming higher, he strikes once more. The nerbo draws a line of blood close to her ear, but the spennacchiera holds fast. Again she falls back, and again she comes up, her strength intensified.

Doubled over, wincing, the boy strikes again, and then again, and sees the bloody trail grow. Tears spill down his cheeks. "Only a few meters left!" he cries inside. "Only one blow more." And before the screaming, cursing multitude he deals it.

Bleeding and bewildered, Gaudenzia tries to pass on the outside, but Giorgio blocks her. The flag of arrival is just ahead. He lifts his nerbo, this time in the sign of victory, but to the gasps of the multitude she cuts around behind him, knifes her body between Rosella and the fence, thrusts her nose under his

266

upraised arm—to win! By the length of her red-scarred head she wins.

It is over. The duel is done. Giorgio falls sobbing into the waiting arms of the Chief-of-the-Guards. The big man is sobbing, too. "Don't cry, Giorgio. Don't look like that. You *had* to do it. You just had to!"

*Chapter XXXI*

AT THE VICTORY DINNER

It was long past midnight when Giorgio was allowed to enter Gaudenzia's stable in the Contrada of the Giraffa. In his hands he carried a kit containing boric acid, a jar of animal grease, and a piece of linen torn from a once-fine tablecloth.

The mare had been lying asleep, but at the sound of the boy's voice she struggled to her feet. He turned his head away. He could not bring himself to face her. Not even glancing in her direction, he asked permission of the barbaresco to treat her wounds.

With a look of understanding the man nodded his consent. "This Palio must have been for you like a bang in the stomach," he said.

Silently Giorgio tore the length of linen into strips. He sopped several in the solution of boric acid. He wrung them out. He doused them again, wrung them out again.

"How many times you going to do that?" the barbaresco asked. "How is it you can face San Martino, but not her? Some time you got to do it."

Miserable, torn by conscience, Giorgio walked tremblingly toward her. Staring at the floor, still unable to look up, he took one step and then another. He felt himself grown suddenly old and bent under his burden of guilt. He wished the distance between them would stretch out and with each step courage would flow into him, but already he was so close he could feel her breath. He closed his eyes, prayed, then forced them to focus on her, and he almost cried, he felt so happy. Even with the red welts she was still beautiful! There was a new quality about her, a kind of spiritual quality, as if she had come through a fire, untouched. Her eyes were fixed on him and they were soft and amber-lit, and the nostrils fluttered and made a little sound, and the ears asked for talk as if this reunion were just like all the others—warm and wonderful and good.

Giorgio gulped. If only she had laid back her ears and come charging at him, or taken a bite through his shirt, fierce enough to show for a lifetime. And though he wanted to sink down upon his knees, and laugh and cry both, and beg forgiveness, yet at sight of the barbaresco watching he went to work like some veterinarian. He washed the cuts across her forehead, and the cross-cuts behind her ear. Then, with the gentlest of fingers, he rubbed the grease into them.

"Gaudenzia!" he said when he had finished ministering. "Now there should be no scars. Those reminders I could not bear. Do you know," he added under his breath, "do you *understand* that you won all by yourself—like the little clay model in Monticello?"

The mare pricked her ears. Whatever it was the boy had said made a nice melody. She raised her head and let out a whinny that bounced back and forth from the stone walls again and again until it faded in a trembly echo. "I bear you no ill will," it said, more plainly than any words.

A few stars were still winking bright and alive when Giorgio left Gaudenzia and walked purposefully to the post office. He had often sent night telegrams for Signor Ramalli. Now he would send one for himself.

The pen on the counter was forked and rusty and the ink lumpy, but the words uncorked themselves like strong wine.

YOUR EXCELLENCE MONSIGNOR
TARDINI. I LOST BUT GAUDENZIA

WON. BY HERSELF. SHE PAID NO
ATTENTION TO ARRANGEMENTS. CAN
YOU ATTEND HER VICTORY DINNER
FOR ONDA NEXT MONTH? SHE WILL
EAT AT HEAD TABLE WITH OFFICIALS
AND ME. IF YOU HAVE FORGOT ME I
AM GIORGIO TERNI ALSO VITTORINO.

The sleepy-eyed clerk squinted out from behind the window of his cage and accepted the message with a loud yawn. As he read it, he snapped sharply awake. "To *Monsignor Tardini*!" he gasped. "Is it *urgente*? And have you the money?"

Giorgio felt in his pocket. "Si, si!" he laughed. "At once it must go."

It was a nice twist of fate that the victory dinner for Gaudenzia's win for the Onda was held in September after her riderless victory for the Giraffa. It made the Onda dinner more important and exciting. Giorgio as her fantino in the first race received a command invitation from General Barbarulli.

And so, on the twenty-sixth day of September, at eight o'clock in the evening, he set out full of eagerness, and in his good suit, for the Contrada of the Onda. On all sides he was met and joined by happy contradaioli going his way.

As he climbed the steep, cobbly streets, an old saying of his father's jumped into his mind. "An end is just a beginning. The dog chases his tail, and that is the way of life; the end and the beginning, they meet!" His mother always laughed then and said the same thing, but not using dogs' tails. "Sunsets are very beautiful sight," she would say, "because they make not an end, but a promise."

The promise was so beautiful it made Giorgio frightened and tremulous with joy at the same time. "It will be that way with Gaudenzia," he thought. "She is only beginning to use her powers, her blood by Sans Souci." He strode faster, passing some of the people who had before passed him. Everywhere people were pouring out of doorways, going to pay homage to a cart horse of great valor. Tonight he was one of them . . . a Sienese. He loved every ancient stone of the city. Nowhere else had he ever felt history as something holy, eternally engraved in stones and in mind and soul.

The Chief-of-the-Guards caught up with him, put a protecting arm around his shoulder. "I bring you two messages," he said in a voice strangely husky. "Affairs of state prevent Monsignor Tardini from attending." He paused and tightened his lips to master his feelings. "And the other news is . . ."

"Yes?" Giorgio felt a cold clutch of fear.

"Your Umbrella Man . . ."

"What about him?"

"Coming here, on his way to celebrate Gaudenzia's victory, he died."

"He—*what?*"

"He got as far as my house, with a beautiful green umbrella for you . . . not oiled cloth, but silk! Real silk!"

Giorgio's throat went dry. He knew he ought to say something, but it was queer how he felt, as if someone had put a heavy hand on his chest and another on his back between the shoulder blades and the two hands pressed and pressed until all the breath was squeezed out of him. Why was it always like this? Why always the joy choked by sorrow?

"Giorgio," the Chief said softly, "do not grieve. Uncle Marco was a very old man. He saw many, many Palios. And he died smiling. 'Tell little Giorgio Terni,' he said, 'tell him that way, way back when he was a knee-high boy, my storytelling begat a very fine fantino!'"

Giorgio listened. As he walked arm-in-arm with the Chief, he put the news in a deep chamber of his heart and drew a curtain over it, not of forgetting but of warm remembrance. The pilgrimage to Onda included the seen and the unseen now.

They had reached the Via Giovanni Duprè, and they both went through the archway and stopped short, transfixed by what they saw. Before them the wavy street, which had given to the contrada its strange name, The Wave, was a mosaic of brilliant lights and colors—glowing, surging, colors—all the colors of the sea when the sun throws millions of sparkles on it. And there, ablaze in front of the noble old church of San Giuseppe, hung

*273*

the Palio banner that Gaudenzia had won! It too was like
the sea, catching all the rays of light and sending them
out again. At its sides two dolphins swam in an ocean
of blue, their tongues spurting living flames. And under
the banner and the sweeping arc of lights, and under the
flags flying, and the flowers cascading from windows
and balconies, hundreds of tables were laid with snowy-
white cloths. But no one was seated. People were milling
about, milling and singing and shouting.

Giorgio suddenly found himself pulled into their
midst, and friends and strangers alike were pumping his
hand and slapping his back and saluting him on both
cheeks. General Barbarulli stood laughing at his bewil-
derment. He beckoned him to the head table, for coming up a side street was Gaudenzia with her barbaresco.

The crowd made a little corridor for Giorgio to pass, and another for Gaudenzia, so that soon they would meet at the head table. But Giorgio arrived first and he saw her coming toward him with that wonderfully long stride of hers. She looked more like a painting than real, with the embroidered velvet horsecloth thrown over her body and the blue-and-white plumes nodding in her headstall. But what made his heart leap was that her scars did not show!

Nearby and far off, the contradaioli shouted, "Behold our Queen!" And in their fervor they rushed to kiss her, to fling their arms about her, but she flattened her ears and laid her teeth bare. The crowd applauded, admiring her spirit. "Let her fantino greet her for us," an old man called out.

Giorgio went to her, and eye to clear eye was threaded.

For a long second he let her snuff the quiet of his hands. Then with her barbaresco he accompanied her to the manger at the head table. It was brimful of oats, with apples and carrots sliced in among the plump kernels. Knowing her love of salt, he picked up a shaker from the table and salted her dinner well.

"Buon appetito!" someone cried, and immediately Gaudenzia plunged her muzzle into the manger as if she understood the toast.

Joy rose to incredible heights. Fingers that failed to touch Gaudenzia now reached out and touched Giorgio as he took his place between Captain Tortorelli and the General.

At last the feast that was weeks in the preparing was brought in—plates of antipasto, platters of steaming chicken, and bowls of spaghetti in meat sauce. It surprised Giorgio that he was heaping his plate high, eating with gusto, and singing between mouthfuls, singing at the top of his lungs.

"Of you we are proud!" the General beamed. "You eat and sing for the Umbrella Man, too. He was a fine eater, that one."

The speeches came next. Long ones, short ones. But Giorgio enjoyed most the tributes addressed to Gaudenzia directly: "Thank you, Gaudenzia, for the beautiful Palio you have conquered for us; for the rewarding of our secret, tenacious belief in you. Have your sensitive ears heard the saying: '*Fate* is Queen of the

Palio'? Believe it not. For now there is a new Queen, and her name is *Gaudenzia*!"

The applause was like a volcano erupting, like a crashing of thunder, like a dike opened in flood time. Giorgio forgot he was at the head table with all the dignitaries. He rose to his feet shouting "Bravissima!" with the populace; "Bravissima, Gaudenzia, the Queen!"

When the roar and thunder subsided, the General grew serious. "The time has come," he said thoughtfully, earnestly, "to reflect upon the ancient yet always new spectacle of the Palio. Already the victory of July seems far away, and already we know the noble results of the August Palio. But," he leaned toward the multitude, his eyes glistening, "in nine months and twenty-nine days the yellow-ochre earth will again cover the cobbles of the Piazza, and again memory and hope will kindle the massive heart of Siena. This Palio is forever written into the archives. Now we turn to a new page."

The victory feast was ended. The band players were striking up once more the sweet, haunting "March of the Palio." People were running toward the banner to kiss it in homage. The waiters were clearing the tables. The barbaresco was leading Gaudenzia away. Giorgio gave the man his moment of glory. Tomorrow would be time enough to call for her from the fine stable of Onda and walk her back home to the Maremma. Yes, tomorrow would be time enough. . . .

The echo of drums accompanied Giorgio as he

walked down into the city for a last look at Il Campo. A harvest moon bulged out from behind the Mangia Tower, washing the palaces in a pale red glow. He listened a while to the fountain playing its tinkly tune in the vastness.

"Nine months and twenty-nine days is not so very far away," he thought. "Why, that is less time than it takes a mare to foal a colt!"

AND NOW . . .

With all of his heart Giorgio Terni believed that Gaudenzia's first victories were only a beginning. And so they were. Proving herself queen, she went on to win the Extraordinary Palio that fall, held in honor of the Marian Year. Giorgio was again her fantino. Thousands of people shuddered as she flung herself at the starting rope, then leaped over it before it touched the ground. From that moment on she won the race majestically, unchallenged. It was her third victory in succession. In all of Palio history no horse had ever done this before!

Strangely enough, Gaudenzia is famed, too, for *not* racing. Because of her spectacular record she was excluded from both Palios in the following year. She was too great a threat to the other contenders. But the next year, in deference to the will of the people, they allowed her to race again. And again she won.

Where is Gaudenzia now? As befitting a queen, she lives in a medieval castle near Siena, one with a history longer than the Palio. In this eventful place where pacts were made and wars were plotted, she has her stable-home. It is big and high-ceilinged, with windows that open wide upon the sweeping hills of Tuscany.

Is she lonely there? Perhaps. But in the months to come there may be a colt for her to nurse, and to teach to race. Meanwhile, she has a hunting dog for company, a groom to exercise her, and visitors from near and far—as far away as America. Most of them she eyes in an aloof and regal manner, permitting none to touch her. She seems always to be looking through and beyond them, looking for a familiar slight-built figure. Sometimes on a Sunday afternoon her looking is rewarded, for among the visitors comes Giorgio, man-grown now.

Nostrils fluttering, she sifts the mixture of scents, sorting and discarding until she finds the right one. Then with a small whicker of remembering, she reaches out to welcome him.

Always their reunion is the same. Giorgio extends his open hand, and after she has licked the salt from it, she playfully nips his shirtsleeve and snuffs his hair. Always it is like this. Never any demanding, "Where were you last Sunday?" Only her eyes holding his, and her ears flicked for the tone of his voice.

"Gaudenzia," he tells her, "the others cannot hold the candle to you. You are still the pride of the Palio, and I'll be back to see you again, maybe in the time of the little fingernail moon or when the moon is full. Maybe both times!"

And usually he is.

*For helping her understand the mystery and meaning of the Palio, the author is grateful to:*

LELIO BARBARULLI, Chief Magistrate of the Contrada
Onda, and his daughter GLORIA, Siena

GIUSEPPE BOSI, guide, Siena

EZIO CANTAGALLI, President of Ente Provinciale per il
Turismo, Siena

TAMI GUROVICH CASCINO, Professor of Literature, Siena

GIORGIO CELLI, Doctor of Accounting, Banca Monte dei
Paschi di Siena

MARIO CELLI, Manager of the newspaper *Il Campo di
Siena,* and his daughter PAULA, Siena

MARIO CHIGIOTTI, Manager of Ente Provinciale per il
Turismo, Siena

ANGELINA CIAMBELLOTTI, President of Centro Italiano
Femminile, Siena

EGIDIO CORSINI, Vicar of the Contrada Giraffa, Siena

MARIO COSTANTI, Castello Medioevale di Bibbiano
Buonconvento, Tuscany

DOROTHA DAWSON, Supervisor of School Libraries, and
JULIA COE, Detroit, Michigan

FINI DEMOLITO, Captain of the Contrada Giraffa, Siena

VITTORIO DE SANTI, Captain of the Contrada Nicchio,
Siena

ETTORE FONTANI, owner of many Palio horses, Siena

BENITO GIACHETTI, Chief of the Guards, Siena

VASCO GIUSTI, Contrada Giraffa, Siena

GIOVANNI GOVERNATO, interpreter and Doctor of
Accounting, Banca Monte dei Paschi di Siena

GUIDO GUIDARINI, official starter of the race, Siena

RUTH HARSHAW, conductor of "Carnival of Books" radio
program, Chicago

VERONICA HUTCHINSON, author and book buyer, Halle's,
Cleveland, Ohio

RICHARD A. KNOBLOCK, Colonel, U.S. Air Force,
American Embassy, Rome

ALDO LENZI, Doctor of Veterinary Science, Siena

KATHERINE LINDSAY, translator, Wayne, Illinois

ALDO LUSINI, editor of the periodical *Terra di Siena*

CONTE GOFFREDO MANFREDI, Rome

TOMMASO MASINI, Secretary to the Mayor of Siena

DELLA McGREGOR, Chief of Youth Services, Public
Library, St. Paul, Minnesota

MARIO NERI, President of Cine Club, Siena

ALFREDO PIANIGIANI, owner of many Palio horses, Siena

VINCENZO RAMALLI, owner of many Palio horses, and his
daughter ANNA, Siena

MARIO ROSSETTI, Doctor of Accounting, Banca Monte
dei Paschi di Siena

NELLO SAINATI, Westchester, Illinois, who vividly re-
created the Tuscany of his boyhood

RENATO SENESI, Manager of the Azienda Autonoma del
Turismo, Siena

ERICA STOPPINI, counselor and friend, and her daughter
MARIA LUISA, Siena

ROBERTA SUTTON, mentor, Chicago, Illinois

DOMENICO CARDINAL TARDINI, Secretary of State of the
Vatican

GIORGIO TERNI, his mother, his father, his sister TERIA
and his brother EMILIO, Monticello Amiata

THE MOST REVEREND MARIO TOCCABELLI, Archbishop of
Siena

ADRIANO TORTORELLI, Captain of the Contrada Onda,
Siena

All the boys of Villa Nazareth and their teachers, Rome

WILLIAM WINQUIST, horseman, Wayne, Illinois

RAIMONDO ZALAFFI, journalist, Siena